SQUAW MAN

Coyote is a renegade Apache who's been butchering a trail along the border for months. But now, with both the US Army and his own people out for his blood, he's ready to retreat into the Sierra Madres — provided his wife is delivered safely to him within the next two weeks. So General Crook hires Carter O'Brien to escort Owl Eye Woman to Coyote. If anything happens to her along the way, though, all hell will break loose . . .

SPECIAL MESSAGE TO READERS

THE ULVERSCROFT FOUNDATION
(registered UK charity number 264873)
was established in 1972 to provide funds
research, diagnosis and treatment of eye diseases.
Examples of major projects funded by
the Ulverscroft Foundation are:-

- The Children's Eye Unit at Moorfields Eye Hospital, London
- The Ulverscroft Children's Eye Unit at Great Ormond Street Hospital for Sick Children
- Funding research into eye diseases and treatment at the Department of Ophthalmology, University of Leicester
- The Ulverscroft Vision Research Group, Institute of Child Health
- Twin operating theatres at the Western Ophthalmic Hospital, London
- The Chair of Ophthalmology at the Royal Australian College of Ophthalmologists

You can help further the work of the Foundation
by making a donation or leaving a legacy.
Every contribution is gratefully received. If you
would like to help support the Foundation or
require further information, please contact:

THE ULVERSCROFT FOUNDATION
The Green, Bradgate Road, Anstey
Leicester LE7 7FU, England
Tel: (0116) 236 4325

website: www.foundation.ulverscroft.com

N

BEN BRIDGES

◆

SQUAW MAN

Complete and Unabridged

LINFORD
Leicester

First published in Great Britain in 1989

First Linford Edition
published 2018

A catalogue record for this book is available
from the British Library.

ISBN 978–1–4448–3556–4

Published by
F. A. Thorpe (Publishing)
Anstey, Leicestershire

Set by Words & Graphics Ltd.
Anstey, Leicestershire
Printed and bound in Great Britain by
T. J. International Ltd., Padstow, Cornwall

This book is printed on acid-free paper

1

Carter O'Brien was fighting mad.

Four men had tried to kill him in the last thirty-six hours. Two of them were already dead. The other two were out there now, in the darkness, and closing rapidly for the kill.

O'Brien wanted to know why.

They'd split up after the first volley of shots. Once they realized they'd been suckered. One of them was off to O'Brien's left someplace. He wasn't sure where. He'd strained eyes and ears for sign of him, but he was good, that one, better than the others. The only reason O'Brien knew he was out there at all was because his partner — who was a lot less professional than he — had snapped a dry twig off to his right, then called out softly, pinpointing the general direction of his friend.

1

O'Brien crouched in the deepest shadows, waiting, his breathing shallow and controlled. He'd been expecting this attack; that's why he'd been ready for it. As a professional fighting man who hired himself out only when the job and the money was right, he accepted such unsociable behavior as what you might call an occupational hazard. But the lead didn't usually start flying until he was on a job, and right now he was between assignments. So who were the murderous sonsofbitches out there now, and why were they so keen to punch his ticket?

O'Brien's .38 caliber Colt Lightning fit his palm like the handshake of a good friend. The weapon was no stranger to this kind of action, any more than he was.

He didn't think they were road agents out for easy pickings. O'Brien was many things — tall, slim, hard-muscled and among the fastest gunmen in the South-west — but rich wasn't one of them. In his plain cotton shirt

2

and wolfskin jacket, creased old cords and worn stovepipe boots, he looked more like a cow-nurse than a gentleman of means. So it definitely wasn't money they were after.

Neither could he think of any grudge-toters he'd run into during the last few weeks. Oh, he'd made enemies over the years, sure. But he couldn't think of many still alive who could afford to send four gunslicks after him.

So who were these hombres?

He had to find out. And that meant he had to take at least one of them alive.

Around high noon of the previous day he'd ridden into a dying little town called Caplock, Arizona Territory, looking to re-supply and wash his tonsils in whiskey. At that time he didn't even know what the place was called, only that it was on the trail to his eventual destination, Fort Bisbee, down on the Arizona-Mexico border.

As he came down out of the low, yucca-studded hills to the north, following the San Pedro River's chuckling course south, the wind began to pick up, blow cold, and heavy black clouds began to gather ominously on the horizon. He entered Caplock's single deserted street just ahead of the storm, eyeing the place from beneath the brim of his tobacco-brown Stetson, saw a saloon, a few stores, small, run-down houses built from rough-hewn timber.

Above him the sky grew steadily darker.

His first stop was the livery stable, where he found and paid a grubby old man to water and feed his appaloosa. That done, he started back up Main, headed for the saloon. He wasn't looking for trouble. Being basically a peaceable man, he never did. But trouble was looking for *him*.

As he hurried up the street, keeping his head down against the wind-driven dust-devils swirling towards him, he heard the thunder's first growl and looked up just as a blue-white streak of

4

forked lightning struck some lonely mountain spot a mile or two away. He reached up to clamp his hat more firmly down atop his close-cut salt-and-pepper hair, moving faster now in order to reach shelter before the rain began.

That was when he realized he was being watched.

Glancing up, he saw two hard cases standing on the porch outside the saloon, lounging the way cocksure men always do with arms folded or thumbs hooked in cartridge belts, heads to one side, insolent, eyes glaring a challenge they just hope you will take up.

One of them was tall, thin and thirty, which made him about three or four years younger than O'Brien. He was dressed cowhand — checked shirt, vest, whipcord pants and high-heeled boots with fancy sunburst spurs — but his gunbelt was a professional's rig, well-kept and housing a double-action handgun.

The man beside him was similarly armed. They were both of the same age and type, although the second man was shorter, tending towards the gut, with red hair, green eyes and freckles.

O'Brien had never seen them before and had no particular desire to ever see them again. He wanted supplies and whiskey, not trouble. The hard cases, however, had other ideas.

Offering them an affable-enough nod, he pushed through the batwing doors and bellied up to the bar. The saloon was a long, dark room sprinkled with tables and chairs. It was empty of people but crowded with echoes. The ceiling was low, the bar-top scratched. Sawdust and cigarette butts crunched underfoot.

There was no booze on display; it was probably kept under the counter. There was a free lunch, however; three soft, specky apples and two curly corned beef sandwiches on a dusty plate. Fortunately O'Brien wasn't hungry.

The forty-year-old bartender looked pale and cancerous. His face was bleached, his moustache thick and black, his eyes blue and sunken. He wore a once-white shirt and armbands, and his smile looked to have been arranged for him by an embalmer.

'Howdy,' he said, placing his meatless hands on the counter.

O'Brien nodded again. 'Howdy back,' he replied. 'You got any decent whiskey around here for a — '

There were two things which saved his life. One was the creaking of the batwings, which told him that the two hard cases were coming back inside. The other was the bartender's suddenly horrified expression, which told him that — for some reason he had yet to discover — they were coming with guns drawn.

O'Brien spun around, saw them filling the doorway and threw himself to one side just as the first shot was fired. He hit the floor in an explosion of sawdust, rolled, came up behind a rickety table with fist around Colt.

His tanned and battered face was oddly calm as he came around the table, not over it, to fire back. After all, there was no time for surprise, no time to ask what or why. No time for anything but instinct.

Overhead a clap of thunder bellowed defiance. The saloon trembled. O'Brien's bullet caught the taller of the two men high in the chest and flung him back against the batwings. He screamed, grabbing at the red wound as his legs buckled beneath him. He fell through the swing doors and collapsed in the street, oblivious to the rain falling like a mourner's tears over his body.

Meanwhile, the second would-be killer — the one with the red hair and freckles — had crabbed sideways, taking cover behind a table just inside the doorway. He fired three shots fast, panicky.

O'Brien used the man-made thunder to change position, moving seven, eight feet to the left. There was no sound now other than the rain pounding the saloon's tarpaper roof and the crash of thunder. A flash of lightning illuminated the shadowy barroom for a second or two.

Red fired again. His shot went wide, striking a small upright piano about ten feet from O'Brien's true position to produce a mad, jangling chord. O'Brien moved fast, triggering two more shots, one to either side of the other man's muzzle-flash.

He heard a soft, choking cough.

Another blaze of lightning; another clash of thunder. The rain came down harder, rattling the windows and battering the town.

Nothing moved inside the saloon.

Gradually one minute stretched into four. Using his left hand, O'Brien reached out, grabbed a chair and overturned it. The clatter came loud, echoing, but drew no response from the man in the other corner.

Another thirty seconds passed. Then the cancerous bartender slowly poked his head above the counter and cleared his throat. ' . . . mister?'

O'Brien kept his faded blue eyes on the far end of the saloon. 'Yeah?'

'I, ah, I think you done punctured that feller permanent, friend. B'lieve I saw him go down the way dead men do.'

O'Brien had seen him go down too. But was he bluffing? Cautiously he straightened to his full six feet two, ready to dive for cover again at the first hint of trouble, but nothing happened.

He crossed the saloon fast, with his Colt pointing the way, then pulled up short. Red lay on his back in the corner, arms stretched out to either side of him. His .36 caliber Navy Starr was still gripped in his left hand. His eyes were wide and glassy. Between them, a single bullet hole leaked blood across his forehead.

With a tired sigh, O'Brien backtracked to the swing doors and peered outside, making sure that Red's buddy was also dead.

He was.

Over at the bar, the skinny barkeep

poured himself a steadying tonic while he watched the freelance fighting-man replace the Colt's spent shells, then set about searching Red's pockets. O'Brien was looking for a reason — or at least a clue — as to why he had suddenly become their target. He found approximately a hundred and fifty dollars in bills and change and a folded picture of a lemon-faced woman in a wide hat — but that was all.

By now the storm, brief but violent as they often were in those parts, was passing over. The still-deserted street was full of broad, mirror-like puddles reflecting the brightening sky as he crouched over the other body. That one, too, carried a fair amount of money but no identification.

O'Brien went back inside. He took no pleasure in killing, never had. It left him tired and spent. But there was no time for rest. He needed answers.

From the bartender he was able to get some information, though not much. The dead men had ridden into town the day before yesterday. At night they'd slept in the livery, by day they'd killed time right here in the saloon. They were mostly quiet, kept themselves to themselves and didn't invite polite conversation, so he'd left them alone.

'But I swear to God, mister, if I'd known they was gonna cause you any grief — '

'Forget it.'

Pausing just long enough to down a much-needed whiskey, the soldier of fortune retraced his steps to the livery and told the grubby old stable-hand to point out the ambushers' saddle-gear.

With the other man watching him curiously, he checked through their war bags with quick, efficient movements, found spare shirts, under-duds, socks, more cash (about fifty dollars), a few supplies (coffee, canned milk, sweetening and jerky) — but nothing else.

With a sigh he regained his feet, peering off into the steaming distance beyond the stable doorway. It was beginning to look as if he hadn't so much killed two men as two question marks.

And talking of question marks . . .

Who are they? And why are they trying to kill me?

It was midnight, thirty-six hours later, and O'Brien was listening to the small, cautious sounds of the bushwhackers moving stealthily through the brush around his campsite. The night was black as sin, the moon hidden behind low cloud. It was so quiet that even his own shallow breathing seemed loud in his ears.

There had been no law to hold him in Caplock, and because he had acted in self-defense, those few townsfolk brave enough to come forward after the shooting saw no point in asking him to stick around while one of them rode sixty-some miles to fetch the county sheriff.

So he'd ridden out of the dying little town a free but puzzled man, wondering if he would ever find the answers to his questions.

The land grew flatter the further south he rode, became largely feature-less desert. Night came quickly and passed just as fast. Then, along about noon today, he thought he'd sighted two riders a mile or so behind him. *Thought*, because one eye-blink later his back-trail was empty again.

Maybe he'd imagined them.

Riding alone for any length of time in such oppressive heat sometimes had that effect on a man.

But what if he *hadn't* imagined them?

Riding on, he tried to figure who they might be. The law? Possibly. But why try so hard to be invisible if they were starpackers? To O'Brien it seemed far more likely that they were friends of the dead men.

So he decided to leave nothing to chance.

Although he saw no further sign of his pursuers — if, indeed they were there at all — he gradually began to stretch the distance between them from a mile to a mile and a half, two miles, two and a half. The sun sank slowly west. Night fell dark and silent. The land cooled off considerably.

O'Brien chose for his campsite a shallow dip of land set well off the main trail, fringed with thick, and in some places virtually impenetrable greasebrush.

Quickly, while instinct told him that he was still alone, he draped his blanket across saddlebags and rocks fashioned roughly into the shape of a sleeping man, built his fire up nice and high and drifted off into the darkness, to wait. Drowned in shadow, he congratulated himself grimly on how lifelike his blanket-wrapped decoy looked in the uncertain light.

An hour passed, an hour of cramped muscles and animal sounds. The fire burned down to embers. An owl hooted. There was a flapping of wings, the small, terrified screech of a desert mouse. Then —

O'Brien's appaloosa stamped, nickered, tugged restlessly at the picket-pin

15

holding it safely tethered some distance from camp. There came a noise, barely discernible. O'Brien tensed. It could have been nothing. But to his trained ear, it sounded a lot like the pumping of a long gun.

Gunfire blasted the night apart then. Hot lead ploughed into the blanket-wrapped shape, tore the dying embers apart to splash orange rain across the scene.

There were so many shots fired in those violent ten seconds that it was impossible to count them, but by O'Brien's estimate there must have been at least twenty.

Somebody sure wanted him dead all right.

When there came no cry or movement from the sleeping figure — not even the instinctive scream or twitch of a bullet-hit victim — the bushwhackers knew they'd been suckered. O'Brien heard a curse, hurried footsteps, knew they'd split up — whoever they were — and were looking for him in order to finish the job once and for all.

He was listening for them now. One of them, as he had already noted, was a real professional. He moved around the campsite like smoke. His *compadre*, however, was little more than hired help; it took no effort to pick out the sounds he made blundering through the greasebrush.

'Hey, Manatee . . . '

The voice came soft, nervous.

Manatee, the pro, didn't reply.

A strand of brush caught on the other man's pants-leg. With a curse he pulled it free. A stray breeze blew up, feeding the fire, and in the light of the growing flames, O'Brien saw him; tall, fat, with a wispy blond moustache and deep, craggy lines etched into his weathered skin. He was about forty or so; in the poor light it was hard to tell. His black hat was pulled low, his sheepskin jacket sensibly buttoned to the throat, his Henry repeater clenched tightly in his big, ugly fists.

He was only about six feet away.

17

Almost close enough to reach out and touch.

He came closer. O'Brien came up out of his crouch, appearing directly in the other man's path. They were so close that O'Brien — a one-time bounty hunter with a damn' near infallible memory for names and faces — was able to recognize him as a rustler, train robber and gun-for-hire by the name of Jim Nelson.

Nelson opened his mouth to yell, but O'Brien wasn't going to have any of that. He lashed out with the Lightning, pistol-whipping the back-shooter hard and fast, without mercy, before he could give their position away to Manatee.

Nelson's eyes rolled up into his head and he went down with a sigh and a rustle of undergrowth. That, however, was all Manatee needed to pinpoint them.

Almost at once the night exploded with another rifle shot. O'Brien joined the unconscious man on the ground, feeling the bullet's hot breath. His eyes raked the area for sign of his attacker, but he saw nothing.

Suddenly there came a crackling of brush; O'Brien caught footsteps, hurrying away. The bastard was making a run for it!

He came up, snap-aimed, fired the Lightning once, twice, again into the night. Manatee — whoever the hell he might be — spun, returned fire.

O'Brien bent low as lead cut the air, fired again, twice, once more. The handgun clicked on empty. With a curse he ejected the spent shells, reloading hurriedly and by feel. Off to his left, the appaloosa began snorting and stamping in panic.

O'Brien snapped the loading gate shut and rose, intending to give chase, then froze as the pounding of a horse's hooves carried to him on the cool night breeze.

Manatee was gone.

But that still left Nels —

Before O'Brien could finish the

19

thought, the fat man with the blond moustache rose up behind him, still groggy from the pistol-whipping, and crashed away through the brush, heading back into the darkness. O'Brien spun, bringing the Lightning up in both hands.

'*Hold it!*'

But Nelson had no intention of holding it. He high-tailed it like a bishop from a brothel.

For one split second O'Brien considered shooting at the fleeing man, then thought better of it. In the poor light a bullet intended to wound might well end up making a kill, and O'Brien needed Nelson alive for questioning. With another curse spilling from his lips, he shoved the handgun back into leather and started after the fat man.

The distance between them closed rapidly. When he judged himself to be near enough, O'Brien threw himself at the running man. They went down together in a chaotic heap.

The fat man rolled over. O'Brien saw

his glassy blue eyes open wide in surprise. Still locked in combat, they rolled over again, so that Nelson was on top.

O'Brien felt sharp stones graze his back through the wolfskin jacket and grunted. Then, in the confusion, he and Nelson were separated.

Wasting no time, O'Brien leapt up onto his feet. As he came up straight, Nelson pulled out a sidearm. O'Brien saw firelight spilling off the long barrel. Without stopping to think about it, he closed in fast, crowding the fat man before he could use the gun.

They wrestled for a while, then O'Brien brought his knee up into Nelson's groin. Nelson screamed and dropped the gun. Then Nelson punched him in the stomach and he doubled over. Nelson bunched his fists and struck him a heavy blow to the back of the neck.

O'Brien went down on his knees and Nelson started to run for it again. In an instant O'Brien was back on his feet.

He went after him and grabbed a handful of his sheepskin jacket. Nelson gave a startled cry as he was hauled around in a tight loop. At the end of the circuit O'Brien waited with his right hand folded into a hard fist.

He struck Nelson on the jaw and Nelson took a wide, drunken step back towards the camp. O'Brien came after him, gave him a left jab that pushed him nearer the circle of light. A third blow sent Nelson back ever further, so that he nearly stumbled over the blanket-wrapped decoy.

The fat man shook his head. Blood sprayed from his nose to sizzle in the fire. O'Brien came in closer just as Nelson pulled a knife. He stabbed at O'Brien's flat stomach and O'Brien danced back out of reach, all the skills he had learned during his spell as a prizefighter now coming to the fore.

Nelson made another lunge. The blade sliced through air. O'Brien grabbed the fat man's wrist and twisted it with such force that Nelson dropped the knife at once. Before he could properly recover his balance, O'Brien gave him a bone-jarring right cross.

Incredibly, the fat man hardly seemed to feel it, just started striking back with a desperate frenzy of blows that took O'Brien completely by surprise. As he tumbled back into the darkness with his ears ringing at the ferocity of the attack, Nelson twisted around to make good his escape one final time.

And fell over the pile of rocks beneath the blanket — to land face-first in the campfire.

He screamed.

Before he could pull away from the searing heat, the flames took away his eyebrows, eyelashes and moustache.

His legs kicked in a mad, spastic dance. His fists pounded the earth to either side of the fire. He rolled, sat up, his screams now escaping from a tender, partly cooked throat.

Bleeding from a dozen cuts and still seeing stars, O'Brien staggered to his feet and back into the circle of light just as the other man began beating at the hungry flames spreading quickly across his sheepskin collar.

Nelson scrambled through the dust in a desperate attempt to outdistance the growing inferno, his legs pumping furiously. O'Brien got a hellish glimpse of the fat man's face; his nose, cheeks, forehead and chin were black, blistered and smoldering.

The stench of burning flesh was overpowering.

Fighting down the bile it brought to his lips, O'Brien reached hurriedly for the blanket, knowing that he had to smother the flames. But Nelson got his feet under him and still shrieking, cut a crazy, stumbling course away from the campsite.

O'Brien, watching the human torch crash blindly through the undergrowth, igniting dry branches every few feet, yelled for him to stay put. He grabbed at the blanket. But as his fingers closed around the coarse woolen cover,

Nelson toppled over, stopped screaming, stopped struggling.

Stopped living.

O'Brien froze momentarily, then hustled through the cold night air until he came to the corpse. The sound that came from inside him was a weary, almost painful moan.

It was easy enough for him to see what had happened. In his tortured flight, the fat man had tripped on an exposed root and fallen to crack his head against a large, sharp rock.

He threw the blanket across what was left of Jim Nelson, killing the flames quickly by starving them of oxygen. Then, unable to fight it any longer, he turned away from the smoking remains and bent quickly to vomit into the darkness.

2

Fort Bisbee was a frankly uninspiring military outpost situated in the desert country around the Arizona-Mexico line, midway between the towns of Sierra Vista and Nogales. O'Brien reached it two days later, summoned by a telegram from no less a celebrity than General George Crook himself.

As with most frontier outposts, Fort Bisbee had no outer wall, so O'Brien had an unrestricted view not only of the log and mud-chinked barracks, shops, stables, sutler's store and guardhouse, but also the adobe-built officers' quarters, too.

As he rode closer, he saw blue-shirted troopers at drill, a few 'kitchen police' peeling spuds in the sunshine outside the mess, a couple of civilians, some copper-skinned Apache scouts. There was some construction going on to the west — it looked as if they were building a chapel. A few other soldiers were working post clean-up duties; half a dozen more were taking arms instruction from a big-bellied sergeant, having to dry-fire outmoded but still accurate Springfield rifles due to the army's chronic lack of ammunition.

Running a forearm across his brow, the freelance fighting man angled his appaloosa towards the C.O.'s office, climbed down and hitched the animal to the tie-rack outside. The building into which he strode had been badly weathered by the surrounding desert, but at least the plain sod roof boasted a ventilator to take away some of the heat which built up inside.

The adjutant seated behind a scrupulously tidy desk was of average height and weight, with the stripes of a corporal sewn onto the sleeves of his dark blue fatigue blouse. He had a round, rugged face, impressive side-whiskers and pleasant brown eyes.

'Good morning,' he said with a nod.

'Can I help you?'

O'Brien closed the door behind him, shutting out the sounds of men and horses at work. 'I'm here to see General Crook,' he said.

The corporal's eyes narrowed skeptically as he studied O'Brien's still bruised countenance. 'Is the General expecting you?'

'Uh-huh.'

'What's your name?'

'O'Brien.'

At once the other man's attitude changed; he became more attentive, efficient. '*Carter* O'Brien?' he asked.

'Yep.'

The corporal got up and came around the desk, extending his right hand. 'Corporal Robinson at your service, Mr. O'Brien. Great pleasure to meet you, sir. We occasionally hear of your exploits, even out here.'

They shook.

'I'm afraid the General isn't here at the moment,' Robinson went on. 'He's off testing our latest acquisition, a

28

ten-barrel crank-revolving Gatling gun. But I'll send a rider out to let him know that you've — '

'That's okay,' O'Brien interrupted. 'Just tell me where I can find him and I'll let him know myself.'

'Are you sure? It's no trouble to — '

'I'm sure.'

The corporal gave him directions to a level stretch of wasteland about a mile or so west which apparently was often used as a firing range. O'Brien nodded his thanks, went back outside, remounted the appaloosa and rode off to find it.

The land surrounding the fort was flat and sandy. Grey sage grew in thick clusters as far as the eye could see, broken every so often by ocotillo, saguaro, cholla and brittlebrush. To the east a series of low, flat-topped mesas rose dun-colored toward the clear blue sky. To the south grew a scattering of smoke trees, prickly pear and pal-overde.

Regular staccato bursts of gunfire

helped him locate the firing range. That, and the clearly discernible wheel-tracks of the Gatling gun and limber. Soon a hundred-foot by fifty-foot oblong of arid land cleared of all vegetation came into view, with a selection of home-made targets at one end and a gathering of soldiers and equipment at the other.

As O'Brien rode closer, the soldiers assumed positions around the repeating weapon. The gun crew comprised a corporal and three troopers. Their audience was made up of a lieutenant, two Apache scouts and, judging from his white canvas suit and cork hat, a civilian.

One of the troopers took hold of the Gatling's handle. Another slid a long, slim magazine filled with ammunition into a slot at the top of the gun. There was a brief, muttered exchange between the lieutenant and his white-suited companion. Then the corporal gave the order to —

'*Fire!*'

O'Brien reined in some distance away just as the first trooper began cranking the handle. Immediately a violent burst of gunfire swept across the plain. The noise was tremendous. The Gatling's revolving barrels belched flame. A hundred feet away, bullets chewed up the targets and spilled them carelessly into the dust. After that — silence.

Muttering nonsense words to calm his skittish mount, O'Brien shook his head, impressed by what he had seen of the Gatling gun's potential. As men and officers crowded around the hot weapon again, discussing various aspects of its performance, O'Brien rode close enough for one of the scouts to spot him. Heeling the appaloosa into a canter, he closed the distance more rapidly, reining in about a dozen feet from the assembled group.

Addressing the man in the white canvas suit, he said, 'General Crook?'

The man stepped forward, peering up at him. 'Mr. Carter O'Brien?' he replied.

'Yes sir.'

O'Brien dismounted and accepted the General's hand in welcome.

'Glad you could make it, Mr. O'Brien. More glad than you know.'

George Crook was in his mid-fifties, with shrewd, close-set eyes, an aquiline nose and a remarkable forked beard the same rusty brown as the hair visible beneath the brim of his cork hat. His was a lean, weathered face, stern and determined, a face that O'Brien found easy to trust. It was the face of a fair if somewhat puritanical man; a face full of character: a face which regularly inspired confidence in both red man and white.

Turning to indicate the much younger man standing a respectful distance away, he said, 'May I present my aide-de-camp, Second Lieutenant William Blevins, late of the Third Cavalry.'

O'Brien nodded to Crook's assistant, a smooth, urbane-looking fellow with dark hair and piercing green eyes.

Blevins was about twenty-five, twenty-six, and something of a popinjay. His uniform was immaculate despite the somewhat withering surroundings, and his boots were virtually free of dust. In O'Brien's book, that alone was enough to make him wary of the second lieutenant.

'Supposed to fire four hundred rounds a minute, so they claim,' Crook said, indicating the Gatling gun. 'But I've never yet seen one that can do the job. I lay blame squarely with the black powder ammunition. It clogs the barrels.'

'So I've heard,' said O'Brien.

Without taking his eyes off the soldier of fortune, Crook said, 'Blevins, have the gun limbered up and returned to the fort, will you? Mr. O'Brien and I will go on ahead.'

'Yessir!'

O'Brien watched Crook stalk off to the soldiers' horses and select a dark, wall-eyed mule from the string. He presented a strange, almost comical figure aboard so lowly a creature, but O'Brien knew that mules were high in his estimation, so wisely he remounted his own horse without comment and soon they were cutting an easy pace back across the sage-scented wilderness, riding side by side in silence.

'Just got in?' Crook asked after a while.

'Yes sir.'

'I expect you'd like some time to wash up and eat before we get down to cases, then?'

'I'd appreciate it.'

'Very well. As soon as we get back, I'll have Corporal Robinson show you where the latrine facilities are and have someone take care of your horse. As for food, perhaps you would dine with me after you've washed up? It would give us the chance to discuss my reasons for asking you out here in more amicable — not to mention private — surroundings.'

'Sure.'

They rode a little further in silence,

until curiosity moved O'Brien to ask, 'Exactly why *did* you send for me, General? Your telegram was a little hazy, to say the least.'

Crook smiled without mirth. 'Because apart from our mutual friend Jim Sundance, who is currently engaged on business elsewhere, you, Mr. O'Brien, are the only man I consider capable enough to tackle the problem with which I find myself faced,' he replied.

O'Brien frowned. 'And which problem is that?'

Their eyes locked across the warm midday air as the General said quietly, 'The problem of averting a veritable blood-bath of an Indian war.'

About an hour later, partway through a lunch of salt pork, beans and cornbread, General Crook said, 'You've heard of the renegade Coyote, of course?'

Having washed away the grime of his journey and donned a fresh shirt for the meeting, O'Brien looked just about human again as he nodded. Everyone had heard of Coyote; the Apache's acts of barbarism had even earned him space in most of the big Eastern newspapers.

'Is Coyote what this is all about?' he asked.

Pushing his plate away, Crook inclined his head. He commanded the Department of Arizona from a permanent headquarters at Fort Whipple, some two hundred miles north and west, so mercifully his billet here at Bisbee — two small, airless rooms that were as dull as they were uninviting — was only temporary.

Just outside the small, square window to their right lay a vegetable garden tended by the wives of officers and enlisted men. Beyond that lay the post trader's compound. Not too far away, O'Brien heard a woman singing — a sweet, gentle sound in an otherwise hostile environment.

'He is *exactly* what this is all about,' the General said. 'But perhaps I'm jumping the gun a bit. Maybe I should explain a little of the background to the problem before I get right to the heart of the matter.'

He was quiet for a while, as he brought order to his thoughts. Finally he said, 'As you are no doubt aware, Mr. O'Brien, the Apache is a proud, warrior race. They live to fight and fight to live. I pacified them once, about twelve years ago — or so I thought. In my naiveté, I actually believed that I could tame their fighting spirit by turning them into sheep men and farmers.

'But I fooled myself as much as I unwittingly fooled the Indians,' he continued with a grim chuckle. 'I ask you, sir, can you imagine trying to raise sheep and crops on the San Carlos Reservation? The place is naught but dust.'

He shook his head sadly. 'You can't tame something meant to be wild,' he said bitterly. 'Oh, you can suppress the natural instincts of these aborigines for a time, certainly, but that is all, Mr.

O'Brien. Just for a time.'

'And time finally ran out?' O'Brien prompted.

Crook nodded. 'About two years ago. A band of Chiricahua, stirred up by a shaman called Nocadelklinny, decided that enough was enough. They jumped the reservation and fled south into Mexico, where they sought refuge up in the Sierra Madres.

'Last September I was recalled from my command of the Department of the Platte to recapture these insurgents and restore peace among the tribes. In May I took a small army of scouts and soldiers across the border and tracked the renegades right up to their mountain lair. Unfortunately there was some bloodshed; nine of the Indians were killed. But eventually I was able to parley with their leader, Geronimo. After our third meeting, the Chiricahuas finally surrendered, and were returned to the reservation.'

He sighed, rubbing at his close-set

eyes. 'There is, however, still the matter of Coyote.'

The General had never been known to smoke, swear, drink coffee or hard liquor, but now he took a deep swallow of strong tea from a cup beside his plate. 'Up until a few months ago,' he said, 'Coyote was among the most loyal followers of the Nednhi Apache, Juh. But rather than return to the reservation with the rest of his people, he and a band of approximately twenty other warriors chose to break away and lose themselves even deeper in the Sierra Madres. As you know, they've been cutting a swathe of terror along the border country ever since.

'As you can imagine,' he continued, 'nothing would give me greater pleasure than to bring this rogue in. Indeed, I am under increasing pressure from both the War and Interior Departments to do just that. But the execution of such a chore is easier said than done. The army is severely undermanned, sir. Whilst deserters are now numbered in their thousands, many more enlisted men lie stuporous in our post hospitals, suffering everything from cholera to venereal disease.'

He shook his head again. 'There is simply no way that I can organize an effective manhunt at this time, and Coyote knows it. But if things go the way I expect them to, we may not *need* to organize pursuit.'

O'Brien frowned.

'Coyote knows that his luck cannot hold forever,' Crook explained. 'Even if the United States Army doesn't get him, there are numerous bounty hunters greedy enough to try and claim the reward upon his head.

'Furthermore, his recent actions have done nothing to endear him to his peers, Geronimo, Juh, Loco and Nana, all of whom are canny enough to appreciate the value of public sympathy and understand exactly what Coyote's display of savagery has done to shift it away from the red man's plight.

'So . . . Coyote has lost much face in

the last few months, and thus has little to gain from continuing to butcher along the border. But what can he do about it? If he surrenders himself to the proper authorities, he will almost certainly be tried and sentenced to hang. If he continues his senseless bloodletting, it is possible that he may even be hunted down by his own people.'

'Seems to me that Coyote's painted himself into a pretty tight corner,' O'Brien said mildly.

'Very nearly,' Crook agreed. 'But there is still one course open to him — *retreat*. Retreat right up into the very heart of the Sierra Madres, never to be seen by white eyes again. And this — through an intermediary — is exactly what he has agreed to do.'

O'Brien pushed his empty plate away and reached for a mug of coffee. 'So what's stopping him?'

'His wife,' Crook replied at once. 'Owl Eye Woman. She has been living at the San Carlos Agency ever since the last of the renegades was herded down from the mountains.'

The General eyed him closely, stroking idly at his forked beard. 'Coyote has made it clear that he will not go until she is by his side, and since he is hardly in a position to collect her in person, I have agreed that she will be taken from the Agency and delivered to him at Cañon Calavera, about fifteen miles south-east of Bisbee, sometime within the next two weeks.'

'And that's where I come in,' O'Brien mused over the rim of his mug. 'You want me to fetch her.'

'Yes.'

'Why?'

The question was blunt, direct; it caught Crook off balance, and before he could properly recover, O'Brien followed it up. 'I know that you're undermanned, General, but I'm sure even you could spare a couple of men to ride down to San Carlos to collect the woman. So why hire a civilian to do the job?'

Crook took another sip of his tea. 'Would you like a list, Mr. O'Brien?' he asked sardonically. 'Very well.' He began to tick off points with his fingers. 'One — the United States Government does not approve of its ambassadors — in this case, me — making deals with renegades. So you're not being hired by the army, sir, you're being hired by me and a few like-minded individuals who see this as the only really feasible way of getting rid of Coyote once and for all.

'Two — Owl Eye Woman *must* have the best possible protection once she is out on the trail, because although this arrangement of ours is secret, there is no doubt in my mind that certain outside influences, of both red and white origin, would like nothing better than for the present hostilities to continue. If something were to happen to Owl Eye Woman, for example, Coyote would go on a killing spree the like of which we cannot even imagine. Any hope of peace would be washed away in a tide of blood.'

He went very quiet.

'And three?' O'Brien prodded.

The General turned his eyes to the small, square window. 'The law states that no Indian may move freely across the country without proper authority. In the case of Owl Eye Woman, that authority could only come if, say . . . ' he returned his gaze to O'Brien. ' . . . if she was married to a white man.'

That was the last thing O'Brien expected to hear. The blood left his face in a hurry. 'You mean . . . ' he began.

Crook nodded. 'Yes, Mr. O'Brien. If you accept this mission — and I pray to God, sir, that you do — you will have to become that most despised of individuals — a squaw man.'

'It's just a formality,' Crook continued as O'Brien allowed the surprise to sink in. 'The marriage itself will be little more than a token ceremony conducted by the army chaplain at San Carlos — one of those 'like-minded individuals' I spoke of. 'Divorce' is easy enough once you reach Cañon Calavera, just a few simple words spoken aloud. Good Lord, man, it's not as if I'm asking you to court the girl, or present a string of horses to her father as a sign of good faith. It's just a . . . well, a formality.'

O'Brien's reply was not immediately forthcoming. He was too busy thinking about the stigma attached to white men who took Indian brides. More often than not they were condemned, shunned, ignored. If he accepted this job and word got around that he'd become a squaw man — even temporarily, in the line of duty . . .

But according to Crook, the deal was secret. With any luck, he might be able to keep it that way.

Slowly his eyes focused again. 'How much are you willing to pay me for this, ah, formality?' he asked bluntly.

'A thousand dollars,' Crook replied. 'That and the satisfaction of knowing that you helped avert a full-scale Indian war.'

When O'Brien still didn't reply, he went on, 'The journey from San Carlos to Cañon Calavera is approximately one hundred miles. Leon Smollett, the Indian Agent at San Carlos and another of my, ah, 'friends', will make sure you're well provisioned.' He paused, eyed O'Brien anxiously. 'Well, sir?'

A quirky smile tugged at O'Brien's lips. 'All right, General, quit worrying; I'll give it a go, God help me. But only because I owe Jim Sundance a favor and happen to agree that this is probably the only way you'll get rid of Coyote once and for all.'

Relief washed across Crook's narrow face. 'Good man! In that case, I suggest that you rest up here today and make a start first thing tomorrow. You don't speak Apache, I suppose?'

'Spanish is all.'

'Very well. I'll have my man Panayatishn ride with you. When you reach San Carlos he can explain everything to Owl Eye Woman.'

It was O'Brien's turn to frown. 'Paya . . . Pana . . . '

'Don't worry about the pronunciation. He also answers to the name of Peaches.'

'Thanks.' O'Brien rose and reached for his hat. 'Just one more thing, General.'

'Yes?'

'Who else knows about this deal you've struck with Coyote?'

Crook had also risen to his feet, and was brushing down his white canvas jacket. Now he stopped and ran grim eyes over O'Brien's face. 'The post commander, Major Watson, Lieutenant Blevins, Corporal Robinson.'

'And that's all?'

'Yes, apart from a couple of friends back East who helped raise the money to pay your fee. Why?'

'No reason. I just wondered how 'secret' this secret really is.'

At the door he turned back. 'Ever hear the name Manatee before?' he asked suddenly. 'Or Jim Nelson?'

Crook gave it some thought, then shook his head. 'No. Should I have?'

O'Brien slipped his hat on and stepped out into the warm afternoon. 'I don't know, General,' he replied honestly. 'I really don't know.'

After breakfasting on chipped beef and toast in the enlisted men's mess hall next morning, O'Brien wandered across to the stables to prepare his appaloosa for the journey to San Carlos.

As he checked through his saddle-bags and war bag, then tested the action of his Winchester 'One In One Thousand' before slipping it back into the sheath buckled to the left of his cracked but comfortable old Texas double-rig, he wondered again about Manatee and the two attempts on his life. Were they in some way connected to his latest job? Was that possible?

On the surface it didn't seem likely, and yet Crook had intimated that someone somewhere had much to gain by keeping the border conflict going.

'Such as?' O'Brien had asked as the General walked him over to the C.O.'s office, where a bunk would be allocated to him for the night. 'What makes you think anyone would want to queer this deal of yours? What would they have to gain by prolonging an Indian war?'

The General had thrown him a troubled sideways glance. 'If you're a white man selling firearms — or fire*water*, for that matter — you've got plenty to gain,' he'd replied in disgust. 'Likewise if you're an Apache who craves glory — the kind you can only achieve on the field of battle.'

That was true, he guessed. But if that 'someone somewhere' was behind the two attempts to stop him reaching Fort Bisbee, how could they possibly have known about O'Brien's involvement even before he'd accepted the job?

Maybe whoever it was had friends inside the garrison. The green-eyed Lieutenant Blevins, perhaps. It was an interesting thought.

The sun was rising fast as he led his

horse over to the C.O.'s office. Leaving the animal tethered outside, he stepped up onto the porch and went inside. Corporal Robinson was at his desk, as fresh-faced and eager as ever; Lieutenant Blevins — the immaculate sonofabitch — was flipping idly through some dispatches in a tray on the wooden filing cabinet.

'Good morning, Mr. O'Brien!' Robinson said, rising to his feet and offering a grin of welcome.

O'Brien touched his hat-brim in greeting. 'The General around?' he asked.

'No, he isn't,' Blevins cut in, turning to offer him a lazy, slightly disdainful smile. 'A reporter from the Chicago *Tribune* turned up late yesterday afternoon. Seems he's doing another of those interminable series of features on life in the Wild West.'

He shrugged, throwing the dispatches back into the tray. 'Well, you know the old man. He's only got to smell a reporter and he's out there aboard that ridiculous mule of his, posing for the camera.'

'Really, lieutenant — '

Blevins spared Robinson the briefest of glances. 'Oh, come along now, corporal. You know how much the General loves publicity.'

Robinson flushed angrily but bit back further comment. 'I, ah, I suppose so. But — '

'It's just that I'm moving out now,' O'Brien said quickly, before the corporal could get himself into hot water by arguing with a superior. 'The General said something to me yesterday about a scout. Paya . . . Pana . . . '

'Panayatishn,' Blevins said effortlessly. 'Ah yes, dear old Peaches. Bit of a surly brute, if you ask me, but his heart's in the right place, and he's fairly good at his job. The General trusts him, anyway.' He reached for his forage cap, hanging on the coat-rack beside the filing cabinet. 'Have somebody find Peaches for Mr. O'Brien, will you, Robinson? If you'll excuse me . . . ?'

'You're excused,' O'Brien replied ambiguously.

Setting the cap at a jaunty angle atop his thick black hair, the lieutenant nodded once, then walked out. O'Brien watched him go, his smile disparaging.

'I'm afraid you really will have to excuse Lieutenant Blevins,' the round-faced corporal said, rising to his feet once again. 'Not all officers are as high and mighty, I assure you. Why, when my turn comes — '

'Don't worry about it, Robinson,' O'Brien replied evenly. 'Now, about this feller Pay — Panny . . . ' He shook his head in exasperation. 'Ah, hell. This feller Peaches.'

Peaches turned out to be a squat, thickset White Mountain Apache of about thirty-live summers. He turned up at the C.O.'s office about twenty minutes later, leading a fine spotted pony by its rein. His face was dark and flat, framed by greasy shoulder-length black hair, centre-parted. His wide mouth was unused to smiling; his glittering eyes, however, were surprisingly animate.

He wore a cheap trade shirt and plain cotton pants inside knee-high moccasins, a breechclout and a cartridge belt with an Army .44 in the pouch. He was bandy, pigeon-toed; only the scarlet headband tied around his forehead identified him as an army scout.

'O'Brien?' he said in a deep, flat tone.

O'Brien, who had been waiting on the porch outside the office, nodded.

'*Inju*. I am Panayatishn. We go to San Carlos, yes?'

'Yes.'

'We will need supplies. It is a long journey.'

O'Brien stepped down and gathered up his reins. 'Not by iron horse.'

Peaches frowned then shook his head. 'You would not know, being white, but I cannot travel by train. It is forbidden.'

O'Brien cracked the Apache a smile. 'You wanna bet?'

Without waiting for an answer, he

swung up into the saddle and Peaches did likewise, mounting smoothly from the right side in typical Indian fashion. Soon there was only a cloud of dust still lingering on the warm morning air to show that they had ever been there.

O'Brien had studied the map on the wall in the C.O.'s office closely before stepping outside to await the arrival of General Crook's favorite scout, and now he led them north-east towards a town called Blackhill, about fifteen miles away. By his reckoning, the Southern Pacific could get them to San Carlos, tucked away in the southeastern corner of the territory, inside a day and a half, two days at the most. From there it was just a matter of getting Owl Eye Woman back to Cañon Calavera, and then waiting for Coyote to turn up and collect her.

At midday they reined in beneath the welcoming shade of a few scrubby smoke trees and slaked their thirsts with warm water from their canteens. They loosened cinches, stretched out on the sandy soil and chewed small, uneven chunks of pemmican sweetened with berries, which the Apache produced from a pannier attached to his crude saddle.

Flies buzzed. Lizards scurried. Around them, super-heated air shimmered.

'You are a brave man, O'Brien,' Peaches pronounced after a while.

The comment surprised O'Brien, and he threw the Apache a puzzled glance. 'Why'd you say that? You don't even know me.'

Peaches shrugged. 'You have agreed to take Coyote's woman as your own in order to transport her freely across the country,' he replied. 'Few *pinda-lik-oyi* would willingly suffer the hatred of their fellow whites by becoming squaw men.'

O'Brien bit off another chunk of pemmican and chewed, tasting buffalo meat and fat. 'You forget,' he said gently. 'I'm doing this for money, Peaches.'

The Apache nodded. 'I know.'

'Then why call me brave when you might just as well call me greedy?'

Peaches' eyes narrowed down as he looked directly into O'Brien's knocked-about face. 'I have heard of you before, many times,' he replied. 'Did you not side the Blind Hawk in the town whites call Fort Smith?'

Again O'Brien registered puzzlement. 'The Blind Hawk?'

'He who also calls himself Ishmael,' Peaches explained.

O'Brien smiled and nodded, understanding. Yes, he had fought alongside Ishmael Hawk, a former Cherokee Light Horse Policeman and just about the most remarkable guide he had ever met; in fact, he still entertained notions of going back into Indian Territory one day to pay the other man a prolonged visit.

'They say you have freed men jailed for life, fought giant bears and entered the spirit-haunted swamps of the Big Thicket. This is so?' the Apache asked.

Reluctantly, and with more than a

smidgen of embarrassment, O'Brien nodded. 'Well, I guess that's one way of putting it.'

'Then truly you are brave,' Peaches said again. 'No wonder the General, whom we call Three Stars, trusts you.'

O'Brien shrugged. 'Well, he trusts you too,' he replied, adopting the Apache's attitude of formality. 'So we have something in common. That said, I think we will get along just fine together, Panayatishn.'

His correct pronunciation of the other man's name surprised him and obviously delighted Pa . . . Pan . . . Peaches.

'Come then,' the Indian said, rising fluidly to his feet. 'We still have many miles to travel before we reach Blackhill. We — '

Abruptly he froze, sniffing at the air.

'What is it?' O'Brien asked, tensing.

'Trouble!' Peaches cried, spinning around. 'Arm yourself, *siquisn!* We are under attack!'

3

Apaches!

There were three of them all told, and they rose up out of the loose earth around the stand of smoke trees like corpses ejected from their graves.

They wore fringed buckskin shirts and matching leggings, war-caps decorated with beads; one sported earrings, another a necklace of bear claws.

Suddenly the air trembled to the sound of their war cries.

Peaches turned just as the first of them stabbed at him with a long, wickedly sharp lance. The scout twisted quickly; the point caught on his baggy shirt, tore the material, but fortunately missed flesh.

Peaches danced backwards; the warrior, caught off balance, stumbled after him. In the same moment that Peaches drew his Army Colt and shot his opponent in the stomach, O'Brien rose up with his own handgun out and took aim on a short, barrel-chested warrior holding a bow of juniper and buffalo sinew five yards away.

His first shot missed. With a curse he shifted his aim and tried again. This time the .38 caliber projectile caught the warrior just below his Adam's apple, shattering the necklace of bear claws and punching a messy red hole through his larynx.

There was just one problem.

In the instant before he died, the Apache loosed his arrow.

It flew so fast that O'Brien didn't see it cross the fifteen feet separating them. He didn't even know that the sonofabitch had fired it until it embedded itself in his left biceps.

The pain was shocking; he couldn't help but cry out and fall onto his back.

Suddenly their peaceful haven beneath the smoke trees became a charnel house, stinking of death. The warrior with the lance lay nearby, his stomach a bloody mulch; the bowman was crumpled a dozen feet away, as still as a picture. Closer, O'Brien could smell the harsh, metallic reek of his own blood, staining the sleeve of his cotton shirt.

He twisted just as their third and final attacker threw himself at Peaches, using a heavy flop-head club to beat the scout to the ground. The would-be ambusher was of medium height, muscular, his coppery face daubed with paint. He struck at Peaches again, catching him on the temple; the scout groaned, releasing his grip on the Colt.

Pausing for breath, his attacker lifted the club for a death blow.

'*Hold it!*'

The sound of O'Brien's voice made him spin to face the white man, who had somehow made it up onto his knees. For one split second their eyes locked. O'Brien looked ashen, felt worse. The other man opened his mouth screamed a curse or an insult, it was difficult to tell which, then launched himself forward.

When no more than three feet separated them, O'Brien shot him point-blank in the chest. The bullet picked him up and threw him down again ten feet away. The Indian quivered for a moment; O'Brien saw the movement of his toes clenching and relaxing beneath the soles of his moccasins. Then he gave a sigh and lay still.

The Apache had been so close to the barrel of O'Brien's Lightning when it went off that there were black powder burns around the ghastly wound in his chest.

A hush fell across the battleground.

Then —

Flies.

The entire exchange had taken no more than a minute. Slowly O'Brien slipped his Colt back into leather, and nursing his injured arm — from which the arrow still projected — called across to his companion. 'Peaches? Peaches — you all right?'

The White Mountain Apache rolled

slowly onto his side and sat up. A discolored bump the size of a large egg had risen on his forehead. As he retrieved his own handgun, he nodded. Then his dark eyes lit on the arrow in O'Brien's arm and he forgot his own pain long enough to scrabble closer.

Inspecting the wound, he said, 'Truly the gods smile upon you, O'Brien. The arrow hasn't gone in too deeply, and unless the tip is barbed, it should pull out easily.' He peered seriously into O'Brien's gray face. 'I remove it now, yes?'

O'Brien swallowed, working up enough spit to say, 'Yes.'

'*Inju.*'

The Apache took a firm hold on the shaft. O'Brien looked away, focusing on some distant point as he tried to think of happier times.

'This might hurt,' the Indian warned.

There was a short, sharp jerk.

O'Brien stiffened; grunted; let out a slow, rasping breath but managed to fight off a merciless wave of nausea just long enough to say two quiet words before finally submitting to a shudder.

'It did.'

Later, after each had patched up the other, Peaches caught and killed a *paisano*, or road-runner, and set it cooking over a small fire.

After a short search, they had found the ambushers' horses picketed just beyond a ridge and set them free. 'Those Apaches,' O'Brien said restlessly. 'They were scouts, right? Army scouts like yourself?'

Peaches turned the small bird on its crude spit. 'You too saw their head-bands, yes?' He nodded, almost to himself. 'Yes. They were Mescaleros. I have seen them around Fort Bisbee once, twice, but I do not know their names.'

'Any idea why they attacked us?'

A rare smile touched Peaches' lips as he glanced up from his culinary chores. 'You saw the gold in their pouches just the same as I did, *siquisn*. It is obvious. They were paid to kill us, my friend. By someone who does not wish us to reach San Carlos.'

He turned the *paisano* again, slowly.

O'Brien scanned the empty horizon thoughtfully, flexing the fingers of his left hand in an attempt to speed up the healing process. He had changed shirts, regained some color, but still his wound ached like a bitch.

'Someone who knew where we were heading when we left Bisbee,' he said, frowning. 'Blevins?'

Peaches shrugged. He did not know; he would not guess.

'Ever heard the name Manatee before?' O'Brien asked.

The Apache ran it silently across his lips, then shook his head. 'No.'

'Damn.'

Every time he mentioned Manatee's name he came up against a brick wall. But it was definitely beginning to look more as if those two recent attempts on his life were connected in some way to his latest job. Which left him with three very interesting questions.

Exactly how did Manatee fit into the picture?

From whom was he getting his information on O'Brien's whereabouts?

And what other little surprises did he have planned for the soon-to-be squaw man?

Before leaving the ambush site, the two men buried the bodies. Then the scout stripped to the waist, smeared cold ashes across his chest, arms and face and set about singing a death chant to the sky god, beseeching him to take the spirits of the dead men into his care.

O'Brien sat his horse some distance away, quiet more out of respect for the ceremony itself than any feelings of guilt he might have had over the death of the three Mescaleros.

Peaches hacked off lengths of his shining black hair, opened cuts on the backs of his hands and forearms, sang at full volume until he was hoarse. Then, he re-donned his shirt, swung aboard his pony and together he and

O'Brien continued their journey.

They were not followed, so far as they could tell.

What remained of the day passed quickly; by the time they reached Blackhill, which proved to be the hub of a predominantly agricultural community, the last of two Southern Pacific eastbounds a day had long since departed. Undaunted, O'Brien and Peaches saw to the comfort of their horses and, having paid the owner of the Neal Street Livery an extra ten cents a head, bedded down in the hayloft.

The following morning they were up with the sun. O'Brien washed in a trough out back, then suggested they find some place to eat.

'You go ahead,' Peaches replied, bathing the lump on his forehead to help the swelling go down. 'I'm not hungry.'

'Sure?'

'Sure.'

O'Brien put his hat on and headed

down to a beanery midway along the main stem, flexing his left arm to alleviate some of the stiffness which had claimed it during the darkness hours. He dined well, stepped back out onto the street much refreshed.

When the 6.45 eastbound rolled in amidst much hissing and puffing thirty minutes later, both men were standing on the plank platform, waiting to lead their mounts up the ramp and into the horse-car.

Although Peaches had forecast some difficulty in obtaining passage aboard the train, the portly conductor gave them no argument when O'Brien stuck a five-dollar bill in his hand. By the time the big Baldwin hauled its cargo out of town fifteen minutes later, the two men and their horses were safely aboard.

Conditions inside the horse-car left much to be desired, however. The atmosphere was stifling and noisy, the car's suspension virtually non-existent, and what little sunlight filtered through the slatted walls barely penetrated the gloom at the centre of the carriage, forcing them to spend the entire journey in a weird kind of twilight. The countryside, by comparison, was resplendent. They rattled through wide fields of cotton and alfalfa, then on across large areas of desert full of ocotillo, saguaro, barrel and pipe-organ cactus.

As one town followed another, so the miles unwound from ten to twenty to fifty. Ten hours later the train dragged itself into a sleepy little burg called Adamsville. It wasn't a town as such, just one last stop-over for the Baldwin to take on water from a giant tank before making its final run into New Mexico and from there up north to Lordsburg, where it finally terminated. But it was in Adamsville that O'Brien and Peaches debarked, because this was about the closest they were likely to get to the San Carlos Reservation courtesy of the S.P.

Now they returned to the saddle,

riding due south across dry alkali flats. The time was a quarter after four, late afternoon but still as hot as midday. They spelled their horses at five, opened cans of beans and washed them down with coffee, then rode on, still trending south. Six o'clock grew into half past. A quarter-hour after that they spotted smoke rising like black string into the still-distant sky; the sooty columns of many cook fires.

Fifteen minutes later they topped a rise and reined in at the sight of an apparently endless sea of wickiups spread across the dusty plain before them. They had reached their destination.

San Carlos.

At first glance, the reservation looked impressive enough to steal breath, but although it stretched across the better part of two million acres, it was not exactly the best patch of land the white man had ever given away. As General Crook had told O'Brien forty-eight hours earlier, San Carlos was little more than dust; a corner of the territory that the white man couldn't use and didn't want.

Back in the '70's, Crook had tried to teach the Apache how to irrigate this barren land and raise crops; O'Brien saw a yellow-green field of corn lifting away to the east, but little more in the way of agriculture than that. For the most part it remained a thirsty wilderness, forsaken by God; a poor, dry, monotonous landscape.

The Apache *rancheria* shelved away to the south, eventually losing itself in the twilit distance. Line upon line of wickiups — crude but hardy dwellings constructed from brush, animal skins and blankets — rose in one jagged line after another, appearing for all the world like the storm-tossed waves of a frozen sea in the deep crimson sunset. Squaws busied themselves around cook fires whilst pre-teenage children played together bare-ass naked, as was their custom.

'Come,' said Peaches, putting heel to

horse-flank. 'We go find Agent Smollett now.'

They closed the remaining distance at a gallop, their arrival creating a brief stir of interest among the Indians on the outer fringes of the huge encampment.

The women were nearly all plump and unappealing, O'Brien noted with a sinking feeling in his stomach. Still, at least most of them chose to hide their dark and solemn faces beneath wild tangles of shoulder-length black hair. That was something, he guessed. Thin, much-repaired blouses and skirts hid them from neck to ankles; some wore long, colorful strings of beads for decoration, others large earrings.

Their men, almost without exception, were a sullen bunch, dressed much the same as Peaches in plain shirts, cotton drawers and knee-high moccasins. All wore government identification tags around their necks. They looked pitiful, O'Brien thought, returning their curious stares as he rode on. Pitiful and somehow lackluster. They were dead men who didn't have sense enough to lay down and get buried, and yet he sensed something else about them, too, something that made him feel vaguely uneasy — a threat of danger, the kind of warning a cornered rat or a rabid wolf will give out.

These men, these warriors, had been pushed around for long enough. One more shove and they were just apt to explode.

O'Brien felt an itch begin between his shoulder blades.

'*Hola*, Panayatishn!'

Peaches twisted in the saddle, returned a wave, called something back in his native tongue, rode on. The Indian Agency itself turned out to be a fairly small dwelling built from imported unpeeled logs. An equally stout storage cabin had been built on at the side, of medium size and windowless, its heavy oak door padlocked against would-be thieves. There was a wide front yard, a barn in good repair, a few Indians doing odd jobs about the place.

Just a little way along from the Agency sat a small but neat church.

O'Brien and Peaches reined in before the Agent's cabin and dismounted gratefully. Almost immediately, a fat man in an open-necked white shirt and black pants came out into the dying day to greet them. He was about six feet tall and moved surprisingly light for his size. He was about forty years of age, with a bald pate fringed by sparse gray-black hair. There were thick-lensed glasses over his watery blue eyes and a cyst the size of a baseball stretching the skin just behind his left ear.

He peered at the newcomers a moment, then smiled. 'Good heavens, it's Panayatishn, isn't it?'

Peaches stepped forward. '*Hola*, Agent Smollett,' he replied gravely, bringing his right hand up to his chest, then around, palm out.

'And you, sir,' the Indian Agent said, turning his magnified eyes to O'Brien, 'must be the man General Crook wired me about.'

'The *squaw* man,' O'Brien replied with a quirky smile. 'Pleased to meet you, Smollett.'

The Agent's handshake was firm and dependable, his manner affable and direct. 'Come along inside, my friends! I was just about to dish up some stew. Not much meat in it, I'm afraid, but at least it's warm and filling.'

'Thanks,' said O'Brien, but Peaches remained where he was.

Smollett frowned down at him. 'How about you, Panayatishn? You too are welcome.'

The Apache shook his head and glanced back at the saw-toothed wicki-ups standing dim in the poor light of fast-coming evening. 'No. It has been many moons since last we spoke, Agent Smollett — but it has been many more since I last saw my woman.'

'Of course, of course! Then let us detain you no longer, *siquisn!*'

Peaches glanced up at O'Brien. 'We

will talk with Owl Eye Woman tomorrow, yes?'

O'Brien nodded. 'Here, at sun-up. Oh, and one other thing, Peaches. You think you could look in on Owl Eye Woman, wherever she is, make sure she's, ah, safe?'

'No need,' Smollett interrupted. 'I've had one of Coyote's brothers and a handful of his cousins standing guard on her for weeks now. Believe me, she's as safe as houses.'

'Thanks. All right, Peaches — see you in the morning.'

Without another word, the Apache remounted his pony and at a light pressure from his knees, the animal spun around and galloped off. O'Brien watched him go as Smollett called a young Indian over to take care of their white guest's appaloosa.

Smollett's home, such as it was, held little in the way of personal comforts. There was an old grandfather clock in the corner with a yellowed face and scratched Roman numerals, a narrow, neatly-made cot, a table, some chairs. Half a dozen books sat lonely on a shelf above the bed; a Currier & Ives print offered one single patch of decoration. In the dull glow of a kerosene lamp hanging from a hook in the low ceiling, the place appeared drab, cheerless, slightly depressing.

'Sit down, Mr. O'Brien, sit down; make yourself at home, as my dear departed mother always used to say. You are hungry, I take it?'

'Some.'

'Good, good.'

He ladled stew into two thick china bowls and brought them across to the table, then took an extra spoon from a drawer in the dresser beside the door and handed it to O'Brien. Soon the two men were seated opposite each other, sharing the meal in silence.

After a while, Smollett glanced up. 'I wasn't expecting you quite so soon,' he said.

'We caught the S.P. from Blackhill.'

'Oh.' The Indian Agent seemed a bit

surprised. 'You'll have to excuse me; it's just that I thought the General might have told me as much so that I could have made plans to welcome you properly, instead of being caught on the hop like this.'

'The General didn't tell you because he didn't know,' O'Brien replied, helping himself to a slice of hard black bread.

'Didn't know? I'm sorry, Mr. O'Brien, I don't follow.'

O'Brien swallowed. 'The General believes that someone somewhere wants to keep hostilities between the Apache and the Army going — and they want it so bad that they might even take a crack at this Owl Eye Woman before I can get her to Coyote, right?'

'Yes.'

'Well, in view of all the hugger-mugger surrounding this job, I figured I could do worse than keep my own movements as quiet as possible. Only it didn't quite go to plan.'

'I beg your pardon?'

O'Brien told him about the two attempts on his life before he reached Fort Bisbee and the failed ambush by the three Mescaleros. By the end of it, Smollett had blanched visibly; he muttered, 'My God.'

'Exactly. This 'someone somewhere' has obviously got a spy from General Crook's staff on his payroll. That's how he always knows where to find me.' O'Brien finished chewing and set his spoon aside. 'So, no offence, Smollett, but if it's all the same to you, I'll play this hand pretty close. When I leave here with Owl Eye Woman, not even you will know which route we'll be travelling to meet up with her old man.'

Smollett nodded his understanding. Up close, O'Brien saw that he had a surprisingly smooth skin, clear and baby-pink. His accent and manner were interesting, too — both unmistakably Eastern in their correctness.

'In the circumstances, I don't believe you could follow any other course of action,' Smollett decided, pushing his chair back and rising to his feet. 'Coffee?'

'Thanks.'

While the water boiled, and darkness fell softly across the reservation outside, the Agent lit a pipe and O'Brien rolled himself a cigarette. Later, sitting back in creaky chairs, Smollett outlined some of the problems he faced as practically the only white figure of authority at San Carlos.

'It's not an easy life, Mr. O'Brien, not by any means,' he said through a cloud of pipe-smoke. 'I have to watch out that my Indians don't get their heads turned by unscrupulous traders, dispense annuities from the government — which, I might add, never turn up on time. I balance the budget here, am often called upon to adjudicate in order to settle various differences amicably, I attempt to teach the Indians how to farm this juiceless land, am constantly pestered by transient whiskey-peddlers . . .'

It had been a long, long day and O'Brien had covered a heap of miles. With his belly full of stew and a cigarette relaxing him, he felt his eyelids taking on weight. Even the wound in his left arm had stopped aching at last, although there was still some stiffness in it.

But then, almost before he knew it, he had snapped back to full awareness and was leaning across the table, fixing an urgent gaze on Smollett's startled face.

'What was that you just said?' he asked sharply.

'What? I'm sorry? About the *tiswin* trade, you mean?' The Agent took his pipe from between his teeth and frowned. 'Are you all right, Mr. — ?'

'Yes, yes, I'm fine. But what was that name you said just now? Some *hombre* you caught selling firewater to your Indians last March?'

Smollett thought back. 'Manatee, you mean?' he said at length.

O'Brien sat back and let out a sigh. A

lazy plume of smoke rose from the tip of the cigarette between his fingers to disappear into the shadows above the kerosene lamp. 'That's the one,' he replied softly. 'Manatee.'

'I don't really know much about him,' said Smollett. He had refilled their mugs and was speaking around his pipe stem again. 'I'd heard of him a time or two. The man's a positive scoundrel, if all's to be believed. Not so very long ago he was selling Apache scalps to the Mexican authorities. Then he was chased out of the Indian Nations for selling firewater to the Creeks and Seminoles. The U.S. Marshal's office in Fort Smith is still after him for that, I believe.

'At the beginning of this year, I caught a few young bucks sleeping off the most horrendous binge of *tiswin* drinking you have ever seen in your life, and promptly made a few enquiries. It seems that this fellow Manatee — by the way, I'm sorry but I don't know his first name — just turned up at the

Agency line one day with a wagon-load of this heathen brew. Well, you know what the Apache can be like when it comes to liquor. Almost before I knew it, he was supplying half the reservation on a regular basis.

'Anyway, the next time he was due back with a fresh supply of *tiswin*, a troop of soldiers from Fort Apache lay in wait for him, hoping to trap him as he and his filthy crew crossed the border. Unfortunately, something went wrong, I'm not sure what. There was a shoot-out. Manatee lost two men, the Army half a dozen. Manatee himself got away and we haven't seen him since. Why do you ask?'

O'Brien told him.

'Good heavens — do you think he could be the same man?'

O'Brien shrugged. 'Could be. It's not a very common name.' He took a thoughtful pull at his coffee. 'Can you describe him for me?'

Smollett shook his balding head. 'I'm afraid not. Never got to see him myself.

But I could take you to a fellow who did see him — and pretty interesting you should find him, too.'

Leaving all his tiredness behind him, O'Brien got to his feet and reached for his hat. 'I'd appreciate it, *amigo*.'

Smollett rose with him, reaching for a string tie and a black hat and jacket hanging on a peg on the back of the door. 'All right — just let me make myself presentable and we'll go see what we can do.'

The fellow was called He Who Sees, Smollett told O'Brien as they walked side by side back toward the *rancheria*. He was an Arivaipa Apache and much respected by his celebrated chief, Eskiminzin.

Full dark was upon the land now, the sky starry and cold, and here and there O'Brien picked out faint orange beacons winking at them through the gloom; campfires burned down to pulsing embers.

'For many years, He Who Sees was one of my best Indian policemen,' the

Agent went on, keeping his voice low as they began to follow a weaving course between wickiups, heading right into the heart of the encampment. 'He's a good man, you see, fair-minded and reliable, and not quite as warlike as most of the . . . ' He broke off to glance left and right at the flat, dusky faces of those Apaches who had come to the openings of their teepees to watch their passage.

'I think I get the idea,' O'Brien replied, his skin tingling uneasily.

'He's always been a bit . . . well, otherworldly, I suppose you'd call it,' Smollett continued. 'So much so that the rest of his people have come to look upon him as some sort of shaman. Often he predicts the weather for us, things like that. Sometimes he even tells me when to expect policy changes from the Bureau of Indian Affairs, weeks before they actually come to pass.' He shook his head. 'I must confess that, until I came here, I really didn't believe much in forces beyond nature, but He

Who Sees certainly changed all that. Even more so after General Crook's Sierra Madres campaign.'

O'Brien threw him a glance. He could smell wood-smoke now, and rough, spicy dough baking nearby. He heard a group of children somewhere, noisily enjoying a pre-bedtime gambol, and closer, the harsh, guttural sounds of men-folk holding a conversation.

'What happened then?' he asked.

They passed a tired-faced squaw and Smollett lifted his hat. 'They were up in the mountains, following a particularly narrow trail, when He Who Sees slipped from his pony and fell a hundred or more feet down a shaly slope. Broke his left leg and fractured his skull, poor fellow. Crook's surgeons patched him up and sent him home, but the leg didn't heal the way it should have. He's a cripple now, with the most horrendous and painful limp, and prone to odd blackouts. But his . . . senses, if that's the right word . . . seem to have sharpened. These days he is something of a recluse, tends to stay in his wickiup, and I know you'll laugh, but his nearest neighbors say that he spends his time communicating with the dead.

'Anyway, enough of ghost stories. You wanted to know more about the bold Mr. Manatee.'

They came to a halt about a dozen feet from a moon-splashed wickiup set in a cleared area roughly at the centre of the *rancheria*. To O'Brien, glancing around uncomfortably, it seemed that those same neighbors who believed that He Who Sees could talk to the dead had deliberately shifted their homes as far from his as possible. Only trouble was, the reservation was so crowded that they couldn't move as far as they'd have liked.

'You stay here a moment,' the Indian Agent whispered. 'I'll go and find out whether or not He Who Sees will grant us an audience.'

He went forward to the wickiup's circular entranceway and bent. There followed a soft, brief conversation in

Apache. O'Brien's left biceps started aching again; he rubbed gently at Peaches' crude dressing to ease it. Then the Indian Agent turned back to him and beckoned. O'Brien went over.

'He'll see us,' Smollett whispered.

O'Brien nodded, bent and followed the other man inside. The wickiup was dark and shadowy, lit only by a small central fire. The freelance fighting-man had to squint to penetrate the murky interior. There was not much in the way of decoration, just a scattering of animal hides and a young squaw stirring something smelly in a pot. She did not look up when they entered.

Her man — He Who Sees — was sitting with his back to the wall facing the doorway, his twisted legs thrust stiffly before him. Long black hair framed his cracked bronze face, falling to the shoulders of his yellow cotton shirt. A multi-hued headband held it in place. He did not smile nor shift the direction of his black-eyed, glittering gaze as they sat cross-legged before him on the other side of the fire. It was almost as if he did not even know they were there.

'Thank you for seeing us,' Smollett said graciously, in the Apache way. 'We are beholden to you, *siquisn*.'

He Who Sees looked at them then. He could have been an old, old man or a young one who had known much suffering; in the dimness it was difficult for O'Brien to tell. For a moment he thought the Apache was going to say something, but instead he inclined his head in a curiously regal gesture. Silence filled the claustrophobic confines of the wickiup.

'You want to know about Manatee,' the shaman said at last. His voice was soft, bubbling, the kind of voice a corpse would use if reanimated.

'Agent Smollett here tells me you saw him once, when the soldiers tried to capture him on the border,' O'Brien said.

Again the Apache inclined his head.

'Can you tell me what he looks like?'

Another nod. 'Of course. I came close to him during the time of the fighting. Would that I could have closed my hands upon him and arrested him for his crimes.' He paused. 'Why is it that you ask after this man?'

O'Brien shrugged, twisting his hat in his hands. 'Because I believe he means me harm.'

He Who Sees nodded. 'He does,' he confirmed quietly.

O'Brien stiffened, narrowed his eyes down still further. 'What makes you say that?'

The shaman smiled at last. 'The gods,' he said simply. Before O'Brien could pursue the conversation, he said, 'You wish to know what this man looks like, yes? Very well. I shall describe him.' He paused again, gathering his thoughts. 'He is not a big man, this taker-of-scalps. He is at least one head shorter than Agent Smollett. And his build is slim. I do not think that any man would give him a second glance or consider him a threat — but that is his strength. He is dangerous, this Manatee, and evil. He has seen maybe five and thirty summers, certainly not more. His face is long and narrow, his brow heavy. His hair is the color of sand and worn to the nape of his neck, and his eyes are a mixture of grey and green. That, my friend, is all I can tell you — about Manatee.'

O'Brien picked up on that. 'There's something else you can tell me, though, right?'

Another slow dip of the head. 'Three things, O'Brien. And you would do well to accept them as warnings given by one who knows.' He shifted slightly. 'In the next few days you will learn much of life and much of death. You must beware of a man wearing a blue bandanna, for he means you harm. And you must expect treachery — from one of the long-knives.'

O'Brien frowned. 'Long-knives? You mean a soldier?'

'An officer,' He Who Sees replied, his expression neutral, his tone flat, 'for I see stripes on his sleeves. He too is evil, and I sense much of Manatee's influence about him.'

O'Brien struggled to remain skeptical, but in the face of the calm confidence with which the Apache made his statements, it was difficult. 'Who is this, ah, 'long-knife'? Can you tell me anything else about him?'

He Who Sees shook his head. 'The gods reveal only what they will,' he replied, focusing on the other man's rugged face. 'It is not for me, their lowly servant, to demand more.'

Time appeared to stop, then, or at least slow down considerably as O'Brien returned the shaman's stare. The Apache looked at him, *into* him, and there didn't seem to be a blessed thing O'Brien could do about it. It was only when he sensed movement beside him that the spell was broken.

Then, following Smollett's lead, he too rose to his feet. 'Thank you, *siquisn*,' he said soberly.

He and the Indian Agent stepped

back out into the chilly night air and started away from the wickiup. 'Well?' Smollett asked after they had walked some way in silence. 'He really is impressive, isn't he?'

O'Brien was buttoning his wolfskin jacket against the cold. 'I guess,' he replied distantly. 'Oh, don't get me wrong, Smollett. I don't doubt that he can tell you when it's going to rain, or when Washington's about to clip your budget. I've heard of such things before, many times. It's just that, if I had to choose between a shaman's prediction and my own instincts, I'd go with instinct every time. It's something I understand; something that's got me this far, anyway.'

Smollett's chuckle was short and almost pitying. 'I understand,' he replied. 'But you'd do well to heed this shaman.'

O'Brien glanced across at him. 'Why?'

'Because he really *does* know what he's talking about.' They strode on.

'Think about it,' the Agent said gently. 'When I first asked if he would see us, the only thing I said about you was that you were a friend. And yet when he spoke to you, he called you by name.'

O'Brien made no comment.

'Neither did I tell him why we wished to see him,' Smollett went on. 'But what was the first thing he said to us?'

O'Brien thought back through the conversation, and went very cold as he heard the shaman's soft, bubbling voice in his head, saying again, *You want to know about Manatee.*

The soldier of fortune pulled up sharp. *You want to know about —*

But how could he possibly have — ?

The stamping of Smollett's boots on the Agency porch tore through O'Brien's line of thought. 'Ah, here we are,' the Agent said cheerfully, turning to face him. 'Another cup of coffee, Mr. O'Brien? If you don't mind my saying so, you seem to have gone a little pale.'

4

O'Brien awoke at sun-up next morning feeling nervous as hell. He knew it was crazy but he just couldn't help it. Because today was the day he got to meet his bride. His *wedding* day.

He shivered.

After their strange meeting with He Who Sees the previous evening, the Indian Agent had offered O'Brien the use of his own cot while he trotted off to bed down in the storeroom next door. Now the blue-eyed fighting-man swung up and out of the tangled sheets, dressed, washed, shaved and ran his fingers hastily through his close-cut hair.

A token ceremony, George Crook had told him. And the General's tone had made it all sound so painless. But to O'Brien, who was the most confirmed of bachelors, even a token ceremony was too close to the real thing for comfort.

He was just finishing up his ablutions when Smollett came through the door, scratching gingerly at the cyst behind his ear. The Agent looked bleary-eyed and somewhat disheveled, but as O'Brien well knew, sleeping on a hard plank floor usually did that to a body.

Upon seeing O'Brien up and about, however, Smollett managed a smile. 'Ah, good morning, sir! Sleep well?'

'Passable, thanks.'

The Agent stomped across to the black iron range and set out a frying-pan. 'Breakfast?'

The thought of bacon and beans did unmentionable things to O'Brien's already fluttery stomach. 'I, ah, I think I'll stick with coffee, thanks.'

The Agent chuckled. 'Not feeling *nervous*, are you? My dear fellow, there's no need to worry. Reverend Allardyce won't hang about — the ceremony'll be over in a flash. And then the happy couple can, ah, depart.'

O'Brien had to grin despite himself. 'If I didn't know better, I'd say you were enjoying this.'

Smollett began to busy himself at the range, heating grease. 'Do you know how much excitement the average Indian Agent gets in his lifetime?' he asked. 'Not much. So I intend to make the most out of this. But seriously, O'Brien, it's not as if you're getting married for life. I mean, as far as you're concerned, this should be little more than a job of work.'

'I guess,' O'Brien allowed morosely.

Outside the window, the sunlight slowly began to strengthen and bounce off the dew sprinkled across the little market garden on the other side of the yard. Down the dirt road a way, the reservation slowly began to stretch, roll and come to life as the flaming orb climbed higher.

Halfway through their first cup of coffee there was a knock at the door. Smollett told whoever was out there to come in, it wasn't locked. A moment later the portal swung wide and Peaches came in, his flat, coppery face an unreadable mask.

'Ah, Panayatishn,' Smollet said, rising. 'Coffee?'

The Apache nodded. As the Agent crossed to pour him a cup, he said to O'Brien, 'I have explained your purpose here to Owl Eye Woman and her family. She understands the need for wedlock and accepts it because it is the only way she will ever get to see Coyote again.

'Sadly, her father was not quite so tolerant. He does not trust the white man. He says that if you should try to molest his daughter between here and Cañon Calavera, Coyote will find out and kill you. Slowly. He mentioned something about chopping off your — '

'Panayatishn!' cried Smollett.

O'Brien smiled. 'All right, Peaches, I get the general idea. But the little lady'll be safe enough with me, I promise.' He paused, eyeing the Apache speculatively. 'I don't suppose she speaks any English, does she?'

'A few words. More in the way of Spanish.'

'Well, that's something, I guess. At least we should be able to communicate a little with one another.' He motioned for the scout to pull up a chair at the table. 'As soon as you've had your coffee, go fetch her for me, will you? Then we'll see what we can arrange with this . . . what's his name?'

'Allardyce,' Smollett said, setting a steaming cup before the Indian. 'Reverend Allardyce.'

Peaches brought the cup to his lips and blew. 'There is no need to fetch Owl Eye Woman, *siquisn*,' he told O'Brien. 'She is waiting outside right now.'

'What — ?'

Smollett hustled across his small quarters and opened the door. O'Brien, understandably more than a mite curious, leaned forward in his chair, but from this position still couldn't see whoever stood outside.

The Indian Agent offered a greeting

in the Apache tongue, then stood back so that Owl Eye Woman could enter. There was a pause, a rustle of clothing. O'Brien's stomach tightened as a shadow fell across the plank floor. Then Owl Eye Woman stepped inside and Smollett closed the door behind her.

Bride and groom studied each other frankly from opposite ends of the room. Owl Eye Woman wasn't the most beautiful she-male he had ever seen. A hard, worried life had dulled some of the shine in her wide-spaced black eyes. But if O'Brien had to make a list, she'd have been pretty close to the top.

She was about twenty-four or -five, five and a half feet tall and clad in a full buckskin dress adorned with fringes and beadwork. Sunlight fell across her face in a warm, golden spill, revealing a skin the color of milky coffee. Her nose was long and straight, her lips full and sensual. Her high, pronounced cheek-bones gave her a regal quality and her somewhat haughty manner spoke of much pride, and not a little disdain for those around her.

She wore golden loop earrings and three or four necklaces of the most intricate beadwork, and a colorful yellow headband held her shining, raven-black hair away from her smooth, sloping brow.

To O'Brien she looked like a princess.

But as beautiful as her face undoubtedly was, it was something else about her that drew his attention and brought a curse to his lips.

Smollett, standing beside her, frowned. 'I beg your pardon? What's the matter, O'Brien?'

O'Brien pointed a finger at the squaw. 'That,' he breathed.

Smollett's frown deepened. 'What?' he asked innocently.

O'Brien's eyes narrowed. '*What?*' he repeated blankly. 'Hell, take a look for yourself, Smollett. That's not wind the little lady's suffering from there; it's a *baby.*' His voice rose in volume. 'You hear me, Smollett? She's *pregnant.*'

'General Crook must have mentioned it,' Smollett said without conviction. 'Perhaps the fact just slipped your mind.'

'It didn't,' O'Brien growled with a shake of his head. 'Crook never said a word, because if he had, I'd've told him to find somebody else for the job.'

Peaches and Owl Eye Woman looked from one face to the other as the white men argued. No more than thirty seconds had passed since the woman had made her entrance, but suddenly O'Brien found himself confronting a whole new ball-game.

'Well . . . perhaps he forgot,' the Agent allowed. 'He is in his middle fifties, after all, and older people do tend to forget things.'

'Not George Crook,' O'Brien replied. 'And not things like *this*.' Again he indicated the woman's distended belly, causing her to wrap her bare arms protectively about it.

Smollett shrugged awkwardly and scratched at his cyst again. 'I can't imagine the General deliberately with-holding such information,' he said. 'But since he isn't here to defend himself, don't you think we should give him the benefit of the doubt?'

O'Brien didn't reply.

'I mean,' Smollett went on. 'All right — Owl Eye Woman is pregnant. But surely that isn't the end of the world?'

O'Brien's snort was derisive, to say the least.

'Well, why is her condition such a problem, then? Oh, I grant you she may experience some extra discomfort once she's out on the trail, but surely even you must agree that as a young and fit woman, she can travel just as well pregnant as barren.'

O'Brien leaned across the table so fast that everyone else in the room save Peaches flinched. 'Are you kidding me, Smollett?' he asked angrily. 'Getting this woman to Cañon Calavera in one piece is going to be tricky enough as it is, what with the possibility of Manatee and his crew looking out for us. But supposing something happens to her while we're on the trail, she miscarries or starts getting contractions or whatever the hell it is she-males do at such labor-some times?'

'Oh come now, let's not be alarmist — '

'Who's being alarmist? I'm just facing facts. What's Coyote going to say if his squaw turns up dead as a doornail? You think he's going to wait around long enough for me to explain how his wife died because her water broke out in the middle of noplace and I couldn't get her to a doctor in time?' He shook his head. 'I'm sorry, but I just don't like it, Smollett. I don't know much about such matters, but she looks almighty close to her time to me.'

'Oh, I wouldn't say — '

'No,' O'Brien cut in. 'I don't suppose you *would*. But the fact is that unless I miss my guess, this here woman's all through cooking and just about to dish up.' He raised his eyes to the low ceiling. 'Why didn't Crook take all this into account? Moving her after she's had the baby'd be bad enough, but even that would've made more sense than doing it *this* way.'

Smollett ran a hand across his pink forehead, but before he could reply, Peaches broke in. 'The General explained Coyote's situation to you, yes?'

O'Brien glanced at the Apache, calming down a little. 'Oh, he explained *that*, yeah,' he said with much sarcasm.

'Then you know that time does not favor him. If he is to escape into the Sierra Madres at all, he has to go within the next two weeks, before the Great White Father in Washington increases the reward upon him and makes him a much more tempting target to bounty-men and the like. He has no choice, *siquisn*. None of us do. Owl Eye Woman must get to Cañon Calavera within the fortnight; it is that simple.'

O'Brien sighed, finishing the rest of his coffee in one short-tempered gulp.

'Besides,' the Apache concluded

mildly. 'You have given the General your word, my friend — and I know you would not break it.'

'You wanna bet?' O'Brien replied belligerently. But even before the retort had left his lips, the anger within him had cooled off. No, he wouldn't break his word; he was too honest, dammit.

He set his cup down gently and reached for his hat. 'All right, Smollett,' he said tiredly. 'I'll need a wagon, something light with good suspension, and supplies for a week or so.'

'Of course,' Smollett replied, obviously relieved. 'I'll attend to it at once.'

'Not so fast,' O'Brien said, lifting a hand to halt him. 'There's something else we've got to see about first.'

The Agent frowned. 'Yes?'

'Yes,' O'Brien nodded glumly. 'The, ah, marriage.'

'Oh! Oh, my goodness, of course!'

'And if you'll take my advice,' he added sourly, 'you'll tell your holy man to keep his service short and sweet — just in case the wedding turns into a christening halfway through.'

O'Brien never did get to find out whether or not Smollett passed his advice along, but Reverend Allardyce — who turned out to be a husky, bearded fifty-year-old with a ready smile, a friendly manner and many wrinkles around his grey eyes — certainly didn't waste any time on speechifying when the time for the wedding arrived at noon.

There in the shady confines of the neat little church, he just got O'Brien to take Owl Eye Woman's right hand in his and muttered something about taking this and taking that and not forsaking the other, and before either of them really knew much about it, pronounced them man and wife.

Owl Eye Woman stood there before the modest altar looking generally confused as hell about these whites and their curious customs, while Smollett did his best to translate the gist of it for her. Reverend Allardyce, all through officiating, reached out to shake O'Brien's hand. 'Good luck to you, Mr. O'Brien,' he said warmly. 'I shall remember you in my prayers, sir.'

'Thanks.'

A certificate of marriage was drawn up and signed by all parties; then O'Brien and his . . . no, *the* squaw stepped out through the plain double doors and into the cleared area before the church.

To be confronted by Owl Eye Woman's relatives.

O'Brien froze in mid-step, startled by their numbers. They had formed a large half-circle around the House of God, and stood grim-faced and silent, the young and the old, the male and the female, maybe as many as sixty of them.

No-one said a word. Not even the children and babies stirred. Allardyce leaned close to whisper in O'Brien's ear, 'Do not falter, my son. You must show them no sign of weakness. Remember the Ninety-First Psalm.'

O'Brien looked blank.

' 'Thou shalt not be afraid for the

terror by night, nor for the arrow that flieth by day',' Allardyce quoted.

Smollett was a bit more direct. Indicating the Indians, he remarked, 'You'll have to forgive them if they don't throw any rice.'

O'Brien fought hard to smile and match the Agent's mood. 'Didn't you tell them it wasn't so much like losing a daughter as gaining a son?'

Smollett grinned and clapped him on the shoulder. 'That's the ticket, *siquisn*. Come on, I've had the wagon hauled out and stocked up.'

O'Brien and the squaw followed Smollett through the human barrier back down the well-worn path from the church to the Agency buildings. Behind them, Owl Eye Woman's family shuffled along at a respectful distance. O'Brien found their silence both ominous and unsettling. To break the tension, he said, 'That reminds me, Smollett.'

'Yes?'

'What exactly does this word *siquisn* mean? Peaches used it on me, I used it on He Who Sees . . . '

The Agent laughed. 'It's . . . well, a term of endearment, I suppose. It means 'My brother'.'

O'Brien nodded, wetting dry lips with his tongue. 'How about *inju?* That's another one I've heard more than once since we left Fort Bisbee.'

'*Inju?*' Smollett repeated. 'Oh, that means 'good'. As in 'Well done'.'

'Thanks.'

As they entered the yard, O'Brien began to loosen up. If Owl Eye Woman's people had meant him any harm, or decided to oppose the wedding for whatever reason, they'd have made their move by now, so he took the fact that he was still breathing as a good sign.

Just in front of the Agent's cabin, Peaches was setting the second of two cartons full of supplies in the bed of a reasonably intact old buckboard. Seeing the wagon, O'Brien went on ahead to test its springs. There was an oil-less creaking, but the seat bounced okay. He nodded to himself; it wasn't perfect, but it should be kind enough on the woman.

His appaloosa had been saddled and tied to the tailboard of the wagon; two Agency animals — a sleek dun and a heavy-muscled grey — stood in the traces out front. Feeling vaguely embarrassed, he turned and helped the squaw up onto the seat, then extended a hand to Agent Smollett.

'Thanks for all your help,' he said as they shook.

The day had warmed up something fierce, and Smollett had to pull a handkerchief from his pocket to dab his bald dome. 'No hard feelings?' he replied.

'I guess not.' He turned to Peaches. 'Obliged to you too, Pan . . . ayatishn.' Mentally he heaved a sigh of relief. 'Perhaps we'll meet again sometime.'

Peaches shrugged. 'If the gods will it.'

O'Brien, having removed his gunbelt for the wedding, now unhooked it from his pommel and strapped it around his lean waist, automatically checking to make sure the Colt hadn't been tampered with.

Finding everything in order, he climbed up beside the squaw. He offered her a brief glance but she did not return it. She was too busy looking sad and scared and not at all like the haughty princess of a few hours before.

'Are you ready?' he asked in Spanish.

Her dark eyes came up to him then, and she nodded.

O'Brien took up the ribbons, kicked off the brake and slapped the horses across the ass. The buckboard started forward with a jolt.

While Smollett, Peaches and Allardyce nodded farewells, Owl Eye Woman's people just stood there in the punishing sunlight, staring silently at O'Brien.

It took them quite some time to reach the Agency line, but even when San Carlos finally lay behind them, the character of the land didn't change all that much.

With O'Brien deliberately holding

the speed down to save the woman as much discomfort as possible, the rattling buckboard ate up the miles at a steady pace. Soon great weathered mesas rose high across the wrinkled land, golden and rugged in the sun-glare. Brittlebrush grew everywhere, as did lupine and saguaro.

It was the worst time to travel, the afternoon, when the sun was at its hottest. Even snakes and Gila monsters lay sluggish beneath its oppressive rays. But O'Brien made sure they stopped frequently whenever he spied likely-looking shade, and regularly helped themselves to the lukewarm water in their canteens to keep from dehydrating.

Throughout what remained of the afternoon, Owl Eye Woman made no attempt to communicate with him. It was almost as if she had withdrawn so deep into herself that as far as she was concerned, he had simply ceased to exist.

But at last evening came and

O'Brien, who had spent the last half-mile looking out for a decent place to make night-camp, steered them towards a *tinaja*, where rainwater had collected in a shallow basin of rock and something of a small oasis had sprung up around the high ground.

In silence they set about making camp. The squaw's reticence didn't bother O'Brien especially. *Yet.* But he knew that it would within a day or so. And by his reckoning, they wouldn't reach their destination much before another six or seven suns had set.

He hoped for both their sakes that she would decide to accept the situation quickly.

By the time he had finished seeing to the horses, Owl Eye Woman had built a fire from kindling Peaches had packed for them and opened two airtights of beans. As he came over to the fire and sat across from her, enjoying the warmth now that a chilly moon had claimed the land, she set the opened cans out to heat.

Rubbing at his still-sore biceps, he watched her flawless face in the fire's St Vitus flickerings. Despite everything he had done to make the start of their journey bearable, the day had been hard on her. There were dull smudges beneath her heavy-lidded eyes, and more than once she stifled a yawn.

He was feeling pretty tuckered himself as he turned his attention to their surroundings. Shadows threw a dark blanket across the endless sea of sand to the west. Mesas and sharper needles of rock were just formless blots in the night.

He turned back to the woman and found her watching him. He smiled but she didn't smile back. She did speak, however, awkwardly, in Spanish. 'You have hurt your arm?'

He glanced down at it, unaware that he had still been massaging it. 'A few days ago,' he replied. 'But it's not too bad now. Healing slowly.'

'But it still pains you,' she said. 'It is a muscle-strain?'

'A wound.'

She rose and came round the small fire. 'Here — I will tend it for you.'

Instinctively O'Brien shied away. 'Uh, that's okay. Thanks all the same.'

But still she came forward, her small, rough hands outstretched. 'It could be that the wound needs cleansing and re-binding,' she said. She was probably right, too — it *was* aching like a bitch again.

He tried to submit as graciously as he knew how, unbuttoning his shirt to shuck out of the left sleeve and expose the wound. The woman caught her breath when she saw his torso. It could have been because she was unused to seeing chest-hair, the Apache having little or no body hair of their own to speak of. But judging from the respect he thought he saw lighting her tired eyes, it was probably more to do with the knife and bullet scars crisscrossing his body, mementoes from a dozen or more bloody confrontations in his past.

Gently she unwrapped his arm and

115

inspected the wound. It looked puffed and angry. A frown pleated her coffee-colored brow. 'Arrow?' she asked.

He nodded.

She was silent for a few moments, then sat back. 'The wound is infected,' she said matter-of-factly. 'It must be cleansed properly or else it will go bad. Very bad.'

He gave another nod. 'That's about what I figured.'

'You will need a doctor,' she told him. 'We will pass a white town soon, yes?'

'Maybe. But I was kind of hoping to bypass any towns we might come across.'

'Because you do not wish it known that you have taken an Indian bride?'

He shook his head. 'Uh-huh. Because transporting you from San Carlos to Cañon Calavera is supposed to be a secret.'

With kind fingers she re-bound the sore wound. 'You must not delay, *pinda-lik-oyi*. Unless the poison is

116

drained from your arm, the infection will spread fast in the desert heat.'

'All right,' he replied. 'I'll see what I can do when we reach the next town on the trail.'

As he tucked his shirt back in, she returned to the other side of the fire. 'Come,' she said. 'We will eat now.'

They did.

In silence.

By the middle of next morning, the lush *tinaja* lay three arduous miles behind them and yellow-brown desert stretched endlessly ahead.

The night had passed without incident, but O'Brien had noticed a distinct deterioration in his left arm this morning. It was stiffer than it had been, and the wound — once he had unwrapped it — seemed redder. Whether he liked it or not, it looked as if he had no choice but to find a doctor and have the poison drained as quickly as possible.

Despite such a gruesome prospect, however, the mood aboard the creaking wagon was more cordial today, and

O'Brien was glad. There were times when everyone had to do something they didn't overmuch care for, and when those times came along it was best to dig in and make the best of it. Now it looked as if Owl Eye Woman had decided to do just that.

In the hour before noon, O'Brien spied clouds bubbling up ahead and promptly applied the brake, bringing the buckboard to a slewing halt.

'What — ?'

Before Owl Eye Woman could properly phrase the question, he hopped down from the seat and hurried back to his appaloosa. He dug a bright yellow slicker out of one saddlebag and brought it back to her. 'Here, put this over you.'

She looked down at him. Overhead the sky grew darker.

'Do it unless you want to get soaked.'

She took the slicker and climbed into it, all but lost in its outsize confines. 'What about you?' she asked as the first patterings of the desert shower began to tap at the stiff material.

'Don't fret about me,' he told her, resuming his seat and taking up the reins again. 'I'll dry off pretty soon once the sun comes back out.'

He did, too, for the shower only lasted long enough to plaster his jacket to his body and flatten his hat-brim comically over his eyes. Then the rain had passed over and the sun returned to dazzle them.

Steam began to rise from his clothes and the backs of the horses, and within five minutes man and land looked dry as a bone once more.

'See?' he said.

Almost against her will, she smiled.

The agreeable atmosphere came to an end shortly after they had stopped to slake their thirst and chew down some practically ancient jerky.

'Riders,' said Owl Eye Woman.

Immediately O'Brien twisted around to follow the line of her gaze. They were on a wide, flat plain burned dry of almost all vegetation. About half a mile

119

to the north lay a series of gently rolling dunes; in every other direction there was little save the old cactus or mesa.

In other words, there was no place for them to hide.

O'Brien watched the riders come closer. There were about twelve or fifteen of them in all, heading towards them at a steady gallop, no more than a quarter-mile away now and closing fast. They were white men as far as he could tell at this distance, loaded for bear and ornery as hell.

Owl Eye Woman looked up at him, showing no alarm on her placid face but unable to keep it from her dark eyes. Her question was simple and direct. 'Who are they?'

He shrugged. 'I don't know. But one thing's for sure — there's no way we can out-run 'em.'

'Then — '

He reached out to grip her forearm, attempting to defuse her panic before it could explode. 'Calm down,' he commanded tightly. 'Don't worry, just leave everything to me. *Comprende usted?*'

Their eyes met for one fleeting instant. Then she looked away. '*Si . . . comprende.*'

By the time the first of the riders was near enough to hail, O'Brien was standing beside the stalled wagon, waiting for them with his Winchester held across his body. Seeing his weapon and posture, the leader of the group hauled sharply back on the reins, causing his strawberry roan to skid to a halt and his followers to bunch in an unruly knot behind him.

He stared at O'Brien for a slow ten seconds, then stood in his stirrups and held up his left hand, palm out. 'Hold up there, mister! No need for trouble!'

O'Brien took a step forward, just to show that he didn't care even if there was. 'Then who are you, and what do you want?' he asked.

For a moment or so they evaluated each other across the twenty-yard gap. In the harsh white glare O'Brien saw that the bunch-leader was about his own age, tall and broad, wearing standard range gear and toting a tin star pinned to his buckskin vest.

The men behind him ranged in age from mid-twenties to mid-thirties. Some of them had the look of townsmen about them, the rest of farm- or ranch-hands.

'Name's Charlie Kingold, marshal o' Wildcat,' the starpacker replied, tapping the badge for emphasis.

'Wildcat?'

'It's a town. 'Bout eight, ten miles that-a-way,' the marshal supplied, hooking one calloused thumb south-west. Without waiting for an acknowledgement, he went right on talking, his words addressed to O'Brien but his eyes lingering with obvious puzzlement on the squaw up on the buckboard seat. 'Put up that long gun, mister. This here's a legally-deputized posse, so you got nothin' to fear from us.'

O'Brien maintained his grip on the Winchester. 'Maybe,' he allowed. 'But this is a rough country, marshal. Sometimes a body can't be too careful.'

'That's true 'nough, I guess,' Kingold agreed. He had a pale, narrow face and strangely inanimate blue eyes. There was a shadow of stubble around his humorless mouth and a few curls of black hair escaping from beneath his round-crowned Stetson. 'But all we want is to ask you a few questions.'

O'Brien shrugged again. 'Go ahead and welcome, then.'

'Come far?'

'San Carlos.'

Kingold made a quick calculation. 'You bin on the trail about a day or so, then.'

'About that.'

'Seen or heard anyone else around here?'

O'Brien shook his head. 'Should I have?'

'Could be. Ever hear of Pinto Pete Painter?'

'Nope.'

'Well, he's a rough one, mister, and I don't mean maybe. Just knocked over Sam Twist's place up by Aravaipa Peak, shot and wounded Sam hisself, violated his wife somethin' fierce and got away with close on four hundred bucks.'

O'Brien shook his head again. 'Haven't seen him, marshal. Haven't seen anyone. But happen we do, I'll try and find some way of letting you know. What's he look like?'

The lawman described someone of average height and build with a tanned face, scarred right cheek, jet-black hair and only three fingers on his left hand. 'You see him, he'll be ridin' a little pinto mare, feisty little bastard. That's Pete Painter.'

'Well, it doesn't seem as if he'd be hard to spot,' O'Brien said, his manner betraying nothing of the tension making his guts roll. 'We'll keep a look-out.'

'How about the Indian?' Kingold asked suddenly. 'She seen anything?'

'Nope.'

The lawman mopped his face with a sky-colored kerchief. 'Who is she, anyway?'

O'Brien's knuckles whitened around

the rifle stock. 'What's that got to do with you?'

Kingold shrugged and smiled, putting his kerchief away. 'I don't know. *Yet.*' His smile vanished quickly and his eyes went cold and flinty. 'Who is she?'

O'Brien swallowed. 'She's my woman,' he said quietly.

The lawman leaned forward in the saddle, squinting. 'She *what?*'

'She's my wife,' O'Brien said louder.

A ripple went through the men behind the marshal. It was not a pleasant muttering.

'You tellin' me you're a goddam *squaw* man, mister?' Kingold asked in disbelief.

'I'm telling you the squaw's my wife,' O'Brien replied, fighting hard to keep his temper in check.

Kingold spat onto the hot sand. 'Same diff'rence,' he opined. 'You got a name?'

O'Brien said yes and told him what it was.

'What you doin' way out here?'

He'd been ready for this one; his answer was already worded. 'We're headed south. My brother's got himself a good job breaking horses down around Nacozari. Says he can get me in there.'

'He know you taken yourself an Indian?'

O'Brien nodded.

'An' he's *still* willin' to help you out?' Kingold chuckled harshly. 'Well glory-be. I'll be honest with you, O'Brien. Was it any brother o' mine who took hisself a stinkin' red nigger as his missus, I'd disown him quick as a blink. So I reckon that makes you a mighty fortunate man.'

From the muttering in the background, it seemed safe to assume that Kingold's men held pretty much the same view.

O'Brien felt the blood rushing to his face. But he knew there was no point in telling the marshal to mind his own business. Still, he had to do something. So he brought the rifle around slowly

126

and carefully until the barrel was aimed right at the pasty man's face.

It got very quiet indeed.

'Was I you,' O'Brien told him calmly, 'I'd ride out of here now — while you still can.'

The lawman imitated a goldfish for two seconds, then said, 'What?'

'You heard me,' O'Brien replied, keeping his blue eyes on the move to cover them all. 'You've got a small mind, marshal, but a mighty big mouth. You've insulted me, you've insulted my wife and you've insulted my brother. Care to even it up before you go? Say something about my *ma*, maybe?' His teeth flashed white through the shadow cast by his hat-brim. 'Go ahead.'

Kingold looked sick. 'You crazy?' he asked, a shade higher than intended. 'You figure to take on the lot of us?'

O'Brien shook his head. 'Nope,' he replied evenly. 'But I don't figure I need to.'

The lawman's gaze flickered to the squaw on the wagon-seat. Owl Eye

Woman watched everything through wide, uncomprehending eyes. 'You must love that red nigger real bad to pick a fight with all seventeen of us,' he rasped at length.

'Either that,' O'Brien replied sociably, 'or I must really *hate* worthless sonsofbitches like you.'

He jacked a shell into the breech, causing sweat to pop on the marshal's forehead. There was a stirring behind the man, a restless stamping of hooves.

'Good day to you, marshal,' the fighting-man said pointedly. 'And good luck with finding Pete Painter.'

Kingold sat his saddle for one more heartbeat. O'Brien thought for one moment that he might actually try for his side-arm. But then the marshal jerked on the reins and his roan wheeled around and fairly shot off across the desert floor, heading southeast.

His men held back a moment, saw that O'Brien wasn't going to lower his guard and kicked their animals to speed. Soon all of them were gone, leaving only dust to mark their passing.

5

After the confrontation their mood took a downturn.

While the squaw drew back into herself and sat beside him in silence with her arms gathered protectively around her swollen stomach, O'Brien kept a restless watch on the surrounding terrain, wary not only in case Kingold and his men should double back after them but also in case he spotted Pete Painter, the rapist-thief the posse had been after.

The following half-dozen miles passed quietly and at a snail's pace. The desert stretched on flat and unforgiving. Casting a glance at Owl Eye Woman sometime around four o'clock, O'Brien found her erect but dozing, her bronzed face slippery with sweat. Spying a jumble of rocks about a quarter-mile away, he urged the horses south-west towards it, and by the time the squaw awoke with a start, he had climbed down and was making camp.

The spot he had chosen was ideal for their purpose. Rocks lifted high on three sides, so that they, their wagon and horses were completely screened from the trail. Another feature in its favor was that there was only one way in or out, making the danger of attack from any other direction virtually non-existent.

'Why have we stopped?' Owl Eye Woman asked as she climbed down to the sand, ungainly in her pregnancy. 'Surely it is too early to make camp?'

'You're bushed,' he replied, leading the horses to a sprouting of sickly green vegetation about thirty feet away. 'And anyway, I estimate that we've come a good ten or twelve miles since sun-up. That's pretty fair progress.'

'We should go on,' she insisted. 'While there is still light in the sky.'

But he shook his head. 'No, Owl Eye

Woman. You need rest.' Rather ungallantly, he pointed to her belly. 'Both of you do.'

He made a small fire with the last of their kindling and heated up coffee, then took his Winchester from its scabbard and set it down beside her. She watched him in silence, then looked up into his face. 'Where are you going?'

'To see if I can find a doctor in Wildcat,' he told her gently. 'I won't be long, I promise. But in the meantime, if anyone else but me comes through that gap in the rocks, shoot first and ask questions later. Understand me?'

She did, understanding also his need for a doctor and accepting the situation stoically.

'You want me to show you how to use that thing?' he asked, indicating the rifle.

'There is no need,' she replied proudly. 'I am Apache, after all.'

'All right. I won't be any longer than I can help, okay?'

She nodded.

He checked his gold Hunter. It was almost a quarter to five, about three hours to full dark, if he was lucky. Plenty of time to get to town and back. He mounted the appaloosa, sketched her a salute and left the camp, heading south-west at a gallop.

It didn't sit well with him to leave her all alone like that, especially with characters like Kingold and Painter in the vicinity. Neither had he forgotten Manatee, if it came to that. But his wounded arm had continued to ache throughout the day and he feared the consequences if he left treatment too late. Anyway, he shouldn't be too long. And God willing, she ought to be safe enough in the rock fortress.

Out on the trail, he realized that the appaloosa had been held to a walk for too long. Now the animal made the most of the open range. Before long O'Brien came to the nearest thing he'd seen to a wagon trace for about a week. Half a mile later he found a signpost which read: WILDCAT Pop. 887.

Half a mile beyond that he spotted the first of the town's clapboard buildings. Despite its being the supper-hour, the main stem was still busy in the sun's sinking light. The town itself wasn't much, a collection of weathered shacks and occasional adobe structures which had grown up at the centre of the area's half-dead agricultural and somewhat healthier copper-mining industries.

There was one church, four saloons, an assortment of stores and two hotels, one small, one not so small. O'Brien left his horse at the first livery he came to and set off up Main Street on foot, searching for a medico's shingle.

He had hardly gone more than a dozen feet when a shrill female voice called out, 'Hey, lover-boy! O'Brien!'

He turned, more than a little surprised as a thirty-year-old woman with bleached blonde hair and dark green eyes came up and threw her arms around him. 'O'Brien, you old ram! My

God, it's good to see you!'

A few locals broke stride to glance at them as O'Brien somehow disentangled himself from the woman's embrace. Holding her at arm's length, he inspected her with a mystified frown.

The woman was wearing an emerald-green dress and jacket which accentuated an impressive chest, tiny waist and flaring hips. She stood about five feet three or four, held a small purse and a dainty parasol. The smile she beamed up at him was both cute and bemused.

'I know it's been eighteen months or so,' she said with mock severity, 'but I haven't changed all that much, have I?'

Suddenly recognition struck him and it became his turn to greet her with a hug, awkwardly because of his stiff arm. 'Well, if it isn't Molly Buchanan!' he said into her high-piled blonde curls. 'How's tricks, girl? Got tired of El Paso, huh?'

'Somethin' like that,' she replied.

He'd first met her back in April '81, just before he'd ridden south to spring a politician who'd been framed for murder from a veritable fortress of a prison. It was Molly Buchanan who had been instrumental in helping to save the life of O'Brien's partner, Jake Mooney — and Molly again who had helped him pass four or five very pleasant weeks waiting for his ten thousand dollar reward to come through when all the fighting was over.

'Hell, you know 'Paso,' she told him happily. 'Thirty-odd saloons and just as many dance-halls and cat-houses. I figured I could do without the competition.'

'So you ended up here.'

She nodded. 'By way of Las Cruces, Bowie, Lordsburg and Tombstone. But what brings you to Wildcat?'

'Oh, this 'n' that,' he replied evasively. 'I got some business needs tending.'

'Still layin' your life on the line, huh?'

He chuckled. 'Well, you know me. Never could resist a challenge — or a blonde.'

He didn't think there was much

chance of Charlie Kingold returning to town so soon, but he didn't want to risk being seen on the street, so he said, 'Say, where you working now, girl? I'd appreciate to buy you a drink before I move along.'

'And I'd appreciate the company,' she grinned back. 'See that saloon yonder? The Hair of the Dog?' He nodded, making out a gaudily-painted two-storey structure with oil-paper windows and bright yellow batwings. 'That's the place. I was just headin' across to start work when I spotted you.'

'Right,' he said. 'I'll see you over there inside half an hour or so. I can't stay long, Molly. I got somebody waiting for me outside town. But I'd like to hear all your news now that we've met up again.'

She reached up and kissed him fully on the lips, then offered him a coy little wave and hustled across the street, dodging traffic.

O'Brien watched her go, wiping a red

smear from his mouth. Molly Buchanan
. . . His mind wandered back to those
lazy Texas days and he smiled. Lord,
the things they'd gotten up to . . .

He stopped a townsman and got
directions to the nearest sawbones, and
once he was pointed in the right
direction, found Dr Henry Carroll's
modest surgery above a butchery on
East Street with ease. Within ten
minutes he was stripped to the waist
and trying not to look at the scalpel in
the grey-haired doctor's left hand.

'Hmmm,' Carroll said as he set the
blade to heat at the fireplace. 'Looks
like you got here just in time, my friend.
Infections like the one you got there,
they're the worst. The poison in 'em
just gathers 'n' gathers 'n' gathers,
y'see, and if it's not released it just
explodes, *poof!*, backs up, contaminates
the whole bloodstream.'

He smiled broadly, as if he'd just
dispensed some really happy news.

'Sometimes you can catch it in time.
You'll be glad to hear that in your case,

I believe we have. But a few more days and I'd be preparing to hack off the entire arm, oh yes. And saw-blades being the price they are — '

'Doc,' O'Brien said quietly, 'just get on with it, will you?'

The wound was sliced open without further ceremony. O'Brien gasped at the pain and gripped the edge of the chair with his free hand. The stench that filled the air was nauseous, to say the least. He shuddered, fighting down rising bile.

'There,' the doctor said with much satisfaction some minutes later. 'Now, just let me give it a thorough cleansing with phenol . . . '

Afterwards, O'Brien wasn't sure which had hurt more, the draining or the patching up. But when he stepped out into the cool and golden evening twenty minutes later, his arm felt better, not so tight, so he decided that all the pain had been worth it.

There weren't as many people on the streets now, nor much in the way of horseback or wagon traffic. The Hair of the Dog Saloon, however, was practically overflowing with patrons — a similar mixture to Kingold's posse; farmers and ranch-men, miners and store-clerks.

When O'Brien finally caught sight of her, Molly Buchanan was leaning across the mahogany counter almost directly opposite the batwings, yelling something to a black-haired bartender. She had removed her jacket and the enticing dip of her dress seemed to show off more than it hid. But that was Molly all over, he decided fondly — big and blowsy.

He elbowed his way across to her, smiling warmly. His shadow fell across her and she turned to face him.

But there was nothing of welcome in her expression now, nothing at all. She looked him straight in the eye, shook her head with something like disgust and promptly turned away to resume her conversation with the barman.

O'Brien felt dread settle like a lead

weight in his stomach. She knew. Somehow she'd found out. Kingold must have returned to town earlier than he'd figured, and word of his encounter with a feisty squaw man had gotten round.

But still he felt compelled to reach out, grab her arm and ask, 'What is this, Molly? What's the matter?'

She faced him again then. Under his insistent pressure she had no choice. But there was none of the old affection in her eyes as she hissed, 'Get out of here!'

'Hey now — '

The percentage girl pulled away from him in one sharp and angry movement, her voice rising high. 'What's the matter, O'Brien? Don't you talk American no more? I told you to get outta here! Go on, get back to your precious Apache!'

Her words struck him like an open palm, and having also heard them, the tight press of drinkers surrounding them turned curiously to see what in hell was going on.

O'Brien swallowed. 'I'm sorry you feel that way, Molly,' he muttered softly. And he was. But there was no use in stopping to argue the matter; even less in trying to explain what was supposed to be a secret. He touched the fingers of his good arm to his hat-brim. 'So long.'

She made no reply.

'Hey, is that the guy Sobey was just tellin' us about?' one of the onlookers asked as O'Brien pushed through the throng, heading for the bat-wings. 'The one as took a rifle to the marshal an' his posse?'

'Jesus God A'mighty, he's got a nerve if it is!'

'It's him all right,' said the man called Sobey, who had been one of Kingold's posse-riders. 'Fred — go fetch the marshal!'

O'Brien ignored the buzz of excitement around him and shoved through the swing doors to head up the street toward the livery. He wasn't so much angry with Molly Buchanan as disappointed. But what the hell — how could she possibly guess that his 'marriage' was a marriage of convenience; that it was just a temporary arrangement made in order to get a defenseless red woman from one place to another? She could only judge him by the information she knew to be fact, after all.

O'Brien threw a glance across his shoulder just as the man called Fred followed him out of the Hair of the Dog and started racing down the street in the general direction of Charlie Kingold's office. He cursed. He didn't want trouble so he lengthened his strides, hoping to be mounted up and long gone by the time the bigoted lawman showed up.

Word hadn't spread as far as the stable, so the acne-scarred livery boy was still halfway civil as O'Brien flipped him a coin to saddle the appaloosa. 'And make it quick, will you?'

A broad grin spread across the boy's

fifteen-year-old face. 'In a hurry, are you?'

O'Brien ignored him, peering out through the stable's high double doors. There was nobody on the street that he felt he should be wary of, just a few townsfolk out enjoying the warm evening air.

He turned his attention back to the boy, who was smoothing creases out of the blanket draped across the horse's back with paint-drying speed. 'I said make it *quick*.'

'I'm goin' as fast as I can.'

O'Brien bit off a cuss-word. He'd have saddled up for himself if it hadn't been for his game arm. Irritably he dug out another coin and flipped it across the shadowy, dung-smelling barn. The boy caught that quick enough. 'Well, try going a little faster and see what happens.'

It didn't do him much good, though; no sooner had the boy led the now-saddled animal from its stall than O'Brien heard one of the double doors

144

opening behind him and saw three bulky shadows fall across the plain plank wall ahead.

He turned slowly. Town Marshal Charlie Kingold was framed in the doorway, flanked by the men called Sobey and Fred. Sobey was tall and fair, with a check shirt and brown eyes. Fred was shorter, heavier, with a face full of blood pressure and a dusting of freckles across his broken nose.

Kingold himself had a Cavalry Colt aimed at O'Brien's belly, but almost as soon as O'Brien saw the gun the lawman put it away.

'Well, well, well,' he crowed. 'If it ain't my friend the squaw man.'

O'Brien eyed the marshal levelly. 'Let it go, Kingold. What happened this afternoon is history.'

'You reckon?' Kingold arched an eyebrow and chuckled. To the stable boy he said, 'Get out of here, Martin.'

Once the boy had gone he said to O'Brien, 'You're under arrest, Indian-lover. Get him, boys.'

Sobey and Fred took one step forward but when O'Brien turned to face them head-on, planting his feet firmly, they hesitated.

'You gonna try resistin' arrest, O'Brien?' Kingold asked. 'That's what Pete Painter did when we caught up with him three o'clock this afternoon.' He chuckled again. 'Yep, we found 'im all right, just drinkin' himself to sleep in some dirty little way-station not far from Antosillo. You wouldn't've thought he had a care in the world, way he was sittin' there. Only when we told him otherwise he went for his gun, an' we blew him right into next week, him *an'* his damn' nag.'

O'Brien's face became inscrutable. It had been a long day and it looked like it was just about to become longer. 'I don't want trouble, Kingold, and I haven't done anything to warrant arrest. So back off.'

But the lawman shook his head. 'No way, buster. Get him, boys!'

They were fast and they were good,

the pair of them. But when the chips were down, this was how O'Brien made his living.

Sobey came into range first, dancing like a prizefighter. He swung a left but O'Brien quickly moved back. Sobey followed, threw a right. That missed as well. But while the blond man was off balance, O'Brien used his good arm to reach through his guard, grab a handful of shirt and swing him savagely around, fairly hurling him into the nearest wall.

Sobey struck hard and bounced off, yelping like a dog with his tail afire. Before he could recover, O'Brien snapped his head back with a beefy uppercut that knocked him straight back where he came from, clutching his ruined jaw.

As Sobey crashed into a mess of hay and horse-turds, O'Brien turned his attention to Fred, who was heavier than his partner and looked to have more fighting savvy.

He did, too. His first blow caught O'Brien right on his cauliflowered left ear and knocked him into a row of heavy hanging harnesses.

O'Brien grunted. But there was no time to shove the exploding stars out of his eyes, nor to flex his bandaged left arm in order to lessen the fire coursing through it; Fred closed in too quickly, not giving him a chance.

O'Brien turned fast, blocked a right cross; a left; got in a blow that clipped the other man's granite jaw. Fred moved out of range, then closed for a swift kill, all fists, crowding him.

O'Brien felt blows land to his stomach, ribs, left shoulder, right cheek. The two combatants parted, staring at each other with murder in their eyes. When they clashed again O'Brien got in quick with a series of right-hand-only punches to the other man's belly.

Fred staggered back. O'Brien went after him. They traded more punches. Then Fred managed to do to O'Brien what O'Brien had done to Sobey; he grabbed the blue-eyed fighting-man by his lapels and swung him around in a

148

half-circle, releasing him at just the right moment to ensure that he kept going, going, going until he struck the stable wall.

O'Brien hit with a solid crash, staggered, almost lost his balance. Fred grabbed him from behind, pinning his arms to his sides. O'Brien swore, straining against the other man, but in vain. Fred's grip seemed to be forged from iron.

'Now *that* is what I call resistin' arrest,' Charlie Kingold remarked, sauntering closer and bunching his fists ominously. Some little way to his left, Sobey snorted but remained unconscious. 'Oh boy,' the marshal went on. 'I would purely hate to be in your boots right now, squaw man.'

O'Brien's head had cleared a bit, although his left arm was still killing him. He saw Kingold coming closer and recognized the promise of pain in the marshal's eyes for exactly what it was.

The lawman's first punch struck him

right in the gut and pushed all the air out of him. If it hadn't been for Fred's restraining grip he would have caved in on himself. But Fred held him erect while Charlie Kingold readied himself to dish out some more punishment.

A right cross to O'Brien's jaw snapped his head sideways. Blood spilled warm and salty from a cut inside his cheek onto his tongue. He sagged. That struck Kingold as funny. He laughed. Then he pulled his right arm back for another blow.

O'Brien fought hard to clear his head. He had to time his move just right, and after that he had to put them all out of action damn' fast.

So just as Kingold planted himself in front of the soldier of fortune with his fists bunched, O'Brien lashed out with his right boot, slamming the toe right into Kingold's crotch.

'Aagh!'

The marshal's scream escaped high and ragged. He bent double, clutching at the source of his agony just as

O'Brien brought his head back into Fred's face.

He screamed, too.

Summoning a reserve of strength from God alone knew where, O'Brien spun to face the fat man and followed up the butt with a left jab, a right, another right. Fred cried out, stumbled, twisted around and spilled face-first into the hay. O'Brien grabbed his aching arm and drew in a shuddering breath.

'Bastard!'

He turned just as Kingold clawed his Colt from its holster. The lawdog's face was beet-red and drenched with sweat — but the hand holding the gun was as steady as a rock.

O'Brien dodged to the left just as Kingold's finger whitened on the trigger, but the bullet went wide anyway. The shot started the horses in the stable stamping with fright. Even O'Brien's appaloosa, used to the noise, side-stepped shyly.

Inside the blink of an eye O'Brien

batted the gun from Kingold's hand, hauled him upright and damn' near took his face off with a right cross.

The lawman joined Sobey and Fred on the floor.

O'Brien sagged a little then, when it was all over. He felt as weak as a kitten and sick to death of fisticuffs. Crossing to his horse, he picked up the trailing reins and prepared to ride. Behind him Kingold sniffed wetly, and when he turned to face the beaten man, he found him holding a blue bandanna to his nose.

'You won't get away with this,' the marshal said in a painful gargle. 'Assaultin' a duly depu — '

'Save it,' O'Brien spat coldly. His angry tone ricocheted off the high walls. 'Anything I did to you or your men was in self-defense, Kingold. You bastards had it coming and you know it.'

'You — '

But O'Brien was too tired to stick around and argue about it. With a groan he hauled himself up into the saddle and walked the horse out onto the street. Ignoring the curious throng who had gathered outside, he set boot to barrel and headed out of town at a hard run.

He made it back to the rock fortress inside thirty minutes, by which time twilight was streaked across the sky and the desert terrain was colored silver with moonlight.

The journey from Wildcat had been fast and furious, but without real incident — until O'Brien rode straight into the barrel of his own Winchester, that was.

Pulling back on the reins, he hurriedly lifted one placating hand. 'All right, Owl Eye Woman, don't shoot! It's me!'

The squaw came out of the shadows to one side of the outcrop's single entrance, holding the rifle across her bloated body. O'Brien dismounted and took the weapon away from her, slipping it back into its saddle-sheath.

'You've been okay?' he asked, getting his breath back.

She nodded, her wide, dark eyes scanning his bruised face and watching as he crossed the campsite, heading for the wagon. 'What is wrong?'

He told her in about half a dozen terse sentences, by the end of which he had tied the appaloosa to the buckboard's tailgate and was readying the team-animals for travel.

'We must move on, then?' she asked despondently.

He nodded. 'We've got to, in case Kingold decides to come after us.' His hands moved swiftly over the ribbons, working largely by feel in the darkness. ''Course, he might not. But I'll feel a sight happier once we're out of his bailiwick.'

He paused and turned to her, finding her kicking sand across their small fire and rubbing at her stomach as if to alleviate some kind of pain there.

'You'll be all right?' he asked, trying to play down the urgency in his voice. 'I mean travelling tonight?'

She gave another nod. '*Si*.'

But something in her tone woke fresh anxiety in him. He strode over to her, took her by the arms and stared down into her face. 'Are you sure?'

'*Si*.'

He could see how pain was fighting exhaustion on her moon-silvered countenance and licked his lips, almost afraid of the answer to his next question. 'Is your time near, Owl Eye Woman?'

Cold night silence filled his ears as she swallowed and blinked moisture from her eyes. '*Si*. I . . . think so.'

His neutral expression masked the despair that washed through him. Trouble was starting to pile up. And if she was about to go into labor, the last thing she needed was more bumpy wagon-travel. But what the hell choice did he have? They were damned if they stayed and damned if they didn't.

'Perhaps . . . ' she began in a small voice. 'Perhaps I am wrong. Perhaps I ache inside only because of the miles we have already covered.'

He didn't believe that any more than she did. But she was game to have said it, he thought, as he gave her goose-pimpled arms a squeeze of encouragement. 'Perhaps,' he told her gently. 'Look — we'll move out, try to put as much distance between Kingold and us as we can. But happen you want to stop at any time, or for any reason, just say the word.'

She inclined her head. '*Gracias*.'

When O'Brien coaxed the buckboard out of the rock fortress a quarter-hour later, the desert on all sides was still empty. Good. Chances were that Charlie Kingold was still having his genitals bathed up in Doc Carroll's surgery and wouldn't have the inclination to sit a horse or lead a posse for quite a while.

But how long was quite a while? Eight hours maybe? Half a day?

They rattled slowly across the wide, untilled wasteland in silence. Above them full dark descended and stars shone down through the clear but biting air. Beside O'Brien, Owl Eye Woman continued to massage her stomach as she swayed hypnotically back and forth. After an hour, O'Brien asked her how she was doing.

'*Si* . . . fine . . . '

But she didn't *look* fine, even in such vague light.

'Here,' he said. 'Grab a-hold of my arm and try to sleep. And don't forget — if you want to stop for any reason — '

'I will, *senor*.'

They trundled on, eating up one mile, another, two more, seven. O'Brien kept an eye on their back-trail but saw no-one. Somewhere a coyote howled. Nocturnal birds flew above them. Owl Eye Woman dozed and woke, dozed and woke, one arm interlaced with his. The moon moved with them, sliding slowly east to west across the velvet sky.

Along about daybreak O'Brien found

himself slumbering at the reins and pulled up to splash water across his stubbly face and down his throat. His eyes felt glassy and his back was sore. Owl Eye Woman didn't look much better. Her long black hair hung in matted strands. Her face looked pale, her eyes haunted. When she too had slaked her thirst, they continued trending south-west.

'How far . . . have we come?' she asked.

O'Brien shrugged and cleared his throat. 'About fifteen miles,' he replied. 'Maybe more.'

'Then we are safe now?' she asked hopefully.

'Well, *safer*, if that's what you mean.'

There was a long pause, filled only by the horses' clopping hooves and the rattle-jingle-creak of harness and leathers. 'How are you feeling now?' he asked at length.

Somehow she conjured up a smile. 'All right. The pains, they were . . . just pains. Nothing more.'

Even before she had finished speaking, however, something had caused her to stiffen there on the seat beside him, and a frown appeared to crease her beautiful face.

'What is it?' he asked urgently.

She shook her head, scared and panicky. 'I don't know. I . . . ' Again she stiffened, clutching at her stomach. ' . . . *Madre de Dios!* Stop the wagon, *senor!*'

He did, bringing the buckboard to a halt amidst towering mesas and mile upon mile of sagebrush.

How she managed to climb down from the wagon he never knew, because by the time her moccasined feet touched the earth she was obviously in the most excruciating pain.

As he came around the stalled wagon she stumbled off the trail and nearly fell into a sandy hollow. He caught her, turned her as gently as he could, lifted and carried her further off the trail to a spot shaded by towering rocks. She passed out for a matter of seconds, came to again as he set her down and put his bunched-up jacket beneath her head as a makeshift pillow.

'It is time . . . ' she whispered when her pain-racked eyes finally re-focused on him.

He didn't understand whatever it was she said next, for it was in Apache. The inflection was clear enough, though. It was practically a wail of despair.

'Go . . . ' she told him, lifting one weak hand to wave him away. 'I . . . will . . . *aah!*'

Her eyes closed tightly and her face screwed up.

'I'm not going,' he said, trying to disguise his own panic and confusion. 'You need help, woman!'

'But — '

'Just lay still,' he cut in. 'That's it. That's it . . . '

He drew in a deep breath, trying to organize his thoughts. But he didn't have any thoughts on childbirth to organize. He didn't have a clue what to do, and he doubted if Owl Eye Woman did, either, this being her first. All he could do was take it one step at a time and pray like hell.

'*Aah!*'

She bit back a scream and reached out to grab his left hand. Tears began to flow from her eyes to lose themselves in the hair at her temples.

'All right, all right,' he said, leaning close and softening his voice to what he hoped would be a comforting croon. 'Just calm down, Owl Eye Woman. Everything's going to be fine. I'm here to help you.'

The woman released her grip on him and he took another deep breath to steady himself. He looked down at his hands and saw them trembling. He tried to still them but couldn't.

Damn!

Throwing another glance at the squaw's tortured face, he found her watching him through a blur of tears. 'It is coming,' she lamented. 'And I am going to die.'

He swallowed hard. *Calm down!* he

told himself. *She's relying on you, dammit! You can't let her down now!*

He sat back, ran a hard hand across his face, then reached out to grab hold of the hem of her buckskin dress. 'Excuse me, ma'am,' he apologized, lifting it.

She cried out again. 'It is coming?'

And it was — he thought. But what the hell did he know about it?

'That's it, honey,' he encouraged, not really knowing what to do for the best. 'That's it, girl. Push!'

She dragged in a deep breath of dry desert air and squirmed against the sand. She pushed again. Again. Once more. O'Brien reached forward to wipe a palm across her feverish brow.

'Help me!' she implored.

He was feeling in need of a little help himself. But he pushed the queasiness to the back of his mind and grabbed one of her hands, squeezing it, not believing his eyes as new life slowly began to appear red and wrinkled from between her legs.

'Come on, Owl Eye Woman, you can do it!'

' . . . aah . . . aaah . . . '

'Come on, you're nearly there!'

Her fingers dug into his flesh, breaking the skin, but he was too entranced by the miracle he was witnessing for the pain to register. She continued straining like hell, letting out her breath in a series of harsh, depleting gasps.

Suddenly remembering the Apache word for 'good' or 'well done', and figuring that it might comfort her to hear something spoken in her own tongue, he said, '*Inju . . . inju . . .*'

She choked, sobbed, discolored the sand beneath her.

'*Inju . . . inju . . .*'

And then, an eternity later —

The woman gasped and lay still. Her glazed eyes looked up at the sky, the sun, a single drifting cloud. Somewhere beneath her line of vision, O'Brien hauled in a calming breath of air and forced himself to slice the umbilical cord with his jack-knife.

Silence. The woman felt at peace.

Then she heard the slap. The slap, and the cry.

A few moments later, O'Brien appeared before her looking down into her face through moist eyes of his own. He called her name and she mumbled an acknowledgement. He held the baby out to her.

It was small, smaller than either of them could have imagined. It had a tiny, creased, old man's face and a dark scraping of black hair across its skull. Its brown hands were no bigger than his thumbs.

'Congratulations,' O'Brien told her, laughing like a fool. 'You're a *mother*, Owl Eye Woman! You've got a baby boy!'

6

An hour later, when he judged it to be safe enough to move them, O'Brien carried first the baby and then the woman back to the buckboard and set them both down in the back, the bed of which he had padded with some blankets. The squaw was still weak but the baby was loud and kicking.

Taking the uneven trail at a slow pace, he led them up into the gentle hills ahead, until he found a campsite not far from a sluggish stream which suited their purpose admirably. Acacia and mesquite grew thick along the stream-bank. Higher up the slope sprang greasebrush, brittlebrush, buckhorn cholla and green sotol plants. It was a beautiful spot, rugged and lonesome save for a scratch-work of mouse and lizard tracks, but it offered them water, shelter from the sun and a good vantage point from which to keep an eye on their back-trail.

While the squaw dozed with the naked baby held close against her, O'Brien cleared a cool spot beneath a rocky overhang and draped a blanket across the soft sand, then carried mother and child across to it and lay them down side by side. The woman's eyes were glassy now, and her eyelids were drooping, but just before he turned to leave her alone, she reached up and took hold of his hand, muttering a word of thanks.

''*Nada*,' he replied with a smile. 'Rest now, while I fix some coffee.'

He moved back down the slope, made a small, smokeless fire and set a pan of water and beans to cook. While the water boiled, he unhitched the team-animals and picketed them alongside his appaloosa some little way away, where they could forage among a green splash of sagewort.

By the time he had finished the coffee was ready. Carrying a mug across to the woman, he found she and her baby fast asleep. But he was pleased; the two of them were going to need all the strength they could get in the next few days, so they might as well grab some peace while they could.

Back at the campfire he rustled up some breakfast. By his reckoning they had come about thirty-five miles from San Carlos, which was better progress by far than he'd expected to make. They had approximately nine days left in which to cover the remaining distance to Cañon Calavera and their rendezvous with Coyote, but that was plenty of time for a journey of no more than seventy miles.

Still, they wouldn't be going any farther today — they daren't. The woman needed rest, and barring outside interruptions — namely, Charlie Kingold — he intended to see that she got it.

He ran a hand up across his face and through his short, sharp hair. Talking of rest, he figured he could use a little of his own. In all the excitement of the birth, exhaustion had left him. But now that things had calmed down again he could feel it seeping back in. His trip into Wildcat, the fight in the stable, the all-night wagon-ride and then the birth of Owl Eye Woman's son ... just thinking about it made him feel weary.

He scanned the uneven country below them. Nothing but rock, sage, cacti and sand as far as the eye could see. No sign of human life anywhere, and no sign of pursuit, either. Good.

He dished up bacon and biscuits and ate in silence for ten minutes. Then he stood up, stretched his spine, found a shady spot at the foot of the rocks not far from Owl Eye Woman, and slept.

The next time he opened his eyes he found the little brown baby wrapped in a cloth at his side, staring at him through blind but curious eyes of indeterminate color. Even as he watched, the child's face screwed up as if in pain, and he thought it might start yelling. But then it relaxed and appeared to smile at him, revealing tiny, toothless gums. Like a fool he smiled back, sitting up slowly so's not to frighten the tyke.

Where the hell was Owl Eye Woman? Judging from the position of the sun, he had slept for about six hours and felt much refreshed. It was now around noon, and the sun was directly overhead, beating at the wilderness land with its unremitting heat.

Carefully he scooped the baby into his arms just as Owl Eye Woman hobbled back from the stream, where she had obviously just been washing herself. Her movements were stiff and sore and her posture spoke of much discomfort, but her face had regained some of its freshness and her dark eyes appeared sharper as she smiled down at him.

Without waiting to be asked, she headed for the fire and poured him a cup of java, then set about fixing him some food. She seemed happy enough to do it, too, almost eager in fact, but he rose and crossed the campsite quickly to relieve her of the chores.

'Uh-huh,' he said, lifting her gently and forcing her back to the relative cool of the rocky overhang. 'You need rest, lady. After what you went through this morning, it's *me* that ought to build *you* up.'

'But — '

He would accept no argument. Leaving her sitting up on the blanket with the baby cradled contentedly in her arms, he set a pot of beans to bubble and opened a couple of cans of peaches as a kind of dessert. The afternoon passed slowly, with the dry desert silence broken every now and then by the nameless baby's gurgling wails. But despite the rough conditions of their hillside camp, O'Brien felt those hours to be full of tranquility, and knew that providing he lived long enough, he would always remember this time fondly.

'We will move on again soon?' the squaw asked towards the end of the day. Evidently she was anxious to be reunited with her real husband again, and to present him with his son.

'Maybe tomorrow, maybe the day after,' he replied. The tip of his cigarette showed orange through the lowering light. 'It depends on whether or not the two of you are up to travelling he explained. 'Don't forget, that papoose of yours isn't even a day old yet.' He crushed the quirley-butt out against a rock. 'We still got some rough country ahead of us, much rougher than the land we've already covered. It's going to take a lot out of all of us, so you've got to be as strong as you're likely to be before we can chance moving on.'

'But what about this man Kingold?' she asked fearfully. 'Will he not catch up with us if we stay here?'

O'Brien shrugged. 'Don't worry about Kingold,' he said. 'If he was coming after us, he'd have been here by now.'

'Then we are safe at last,' she said, relief plain in her voice. 'And we have more than enough time to reach Coyote before he withdraws into the mountains.'

He nodded agreement to set her mind at rest. But he was thinking about Manatee, and whatever dangers still lay ahead for them.

Owl Eye woman shook him awake at sun-up next morning, her face full of distress in the watery gray light of dawn.

'Uh . . . what . . . ?'

'*Senor!*'

Her voice was a sharp, insistent whisper that sliced through the cobwebs in his brain.

'*Senor*, hurry! We are being watched!'

He came up from his blanket with the Lightning in his hand, automatically putting himself between the woman and whatever threatened them. But the still-cold desert appeared empty on all sides.

'Where are they?' he hissed.

She came around to stand beside him. 'Th — there,' she replied tearfully, pointing away to the north and east, at a long ragged ridge about three-quarters of a mile away.

O'Brien ran his faded blue eyes along its five hundred yard length, but saw only sage, prickly pear and saguaro. 'You must have pretty good eyesight,' he said mildly.

She shook her head. 'No better than anyone else's. But the air is clear here and does not distort. And in any case, I did not see a person there. I saw a . . . a flash.'

'Flash?'

She nodded. '*Si*. A glint, as of the rising sun reflecting from a magic eye.'

He frowned, telling himself it was still too early in the day for conundrums. 'Magic eye? What do you mean — a spy-glass?'

'Yes, yes, a spy-glass!'

In a few flustered words she told O'Brien that she had been up feeding the baby whilst his sleep still afforded her some privacy, when her attention had been drawn to a series of intermittent flashes

173

of sunlight reflecting — presumably — from some kind of telescope.

'Or field-glasses,' O'Brien said, taking his own battered pair from his war bag.

He put the binoculars to his eyes and raked the ridge once more. Again he came up empty.

How much credence could he place in what she'd told him? Had she really seen something over there, or mistaken something perfectly harmless? She sure sounded convincing, he thought. But perhaps that was because she was still feeling spooked by the events of the last few days, and convinced herself that whatever she had seen was of some menacing origin.

Still . . .

O'Brien was a man who never, ever took chances if he could help it, and he had no intention of starting now. The Lightning was still in his fist. Keeping his narrow gaze on the cacti-studded ridge, he performed a reverse road-agent's spin and handed her the gun butt-first.

'Wait here,' he said, hanging the field-glasses around his neck. 'I'll go take a closer look.'

'But — '

His expression silenced further protest. 'Just do it, Owl Eye Woman.'

As he hauled his Winchester from its sheath and jacked a shell into the breech, he pointed to the gun in her hand. 'Don't be afraid to use that if you have to,' he said. 'It's a double-action, so all you got to do is point it and pull the trigger.'

She nodded her understanding.

'Now, where exactly along that ridge did you see these flashes?'

She pointed. 'There. Midway along, by that cluster of cactus.'

'The tall ones with their arms reaching up?'

'*Si.*'

'Right,' he said. 'Don't worry, Owl Eye Woman. It's probably nothing. I'll be back in a while.'

The sun was climbing faster now, shooing the last grey stains of night from the land, but it was still dark enough for a cautious man to cross the desert floor unseen.

O'Brien was a cautious man.

He did not claim to know everything about hunting and tracking, but he had picked up one or two useful tips on sneaking around without getting caught over the years, and he put them all to good use now.

Saguaro rose like giants through the gloom. Stunted, red-spined barrel cactus lay across the area like droplets of blood. O'Brien skirted them all, alternately crawling then scuttling closer to the ridge. Once he pulled back sharp and swung a wide loop when he heard a sleepy diamondback's warning rattle two or three feet away. Another time he froze with his belly to the ground as an eight-eyed wolf spider made its hairy-legged way across the sand about four inches from his nose.

He made tortuously slow progress across the flatland, feeling and edging his way inch by inch, foot by foot. Then he felt the ground begin to rise beneath him and knew he'd reached the foot of the ridge.

He looked up and got a worm's-eye view of cactus, brittlebrush and ocotillo shelving up to the gradually-coloring sky. Warily he eased up onto all fours. The stand of saguaro Owl Eye Woman had indicated was almost directly above him. But there was neither sound nor movement up there. Not even a breeze disturbed the stillness.

With a sigh he tightened his grip on the Winchester and took hold of his field-glasses to stop them dragging. Then he started up the slope, ready to hug dirt the moment he heard or saw anything suspect from the ridge above.

He made it to the crest without challenge, however, and taking his hat off, peered cautiously over the rim to see what lay beyond.

There was nothing on the other side save more of the same desert he'd already traversed. He checked the terrain in both directions. Nothing else. No-one. He went up and over the ridge fast, so that he wouldn't be skylined any longer than he could help. But it appeared that he had the promontory to himself. Which — if Owl Eye Woman wound up being mistaken — was good news.

Still keeping low, he began to scour the ground around the saguaro patch for tracks, but apart from animal markings he —

He froze.

Suddenly he found himself presented with a number of deep boot-prints, defined sharply enough in the loose soil for him to accept without question the fact that they had been made recently.

So Owl Eye Woman had been right, he thought. Somebody *had* been up here!

He swore.

Casting a wider net, he soon found an empty bean-can, two cigar butts, more boot tracks, shod hooves, fresh horse-apples. Someone had been up here for a good long while. Someone who'd been watching their every move.

One man.

Manatee?

Kingold?

O'Brien didn't know and couldn't guess. All he knew for sure was that whoever he was, he was long gone now.

Or was he?

A faint jingle of harness convinced O'Brien otherwise.

He dodged to one side, seeking cover among some pungent greasebrush, his hands gripping the Winchester with enough force to bleach his knuckles. But no-one challenged him, and when he heard the sound again he was able to pinpoint it more accurately as coming from some distance ahead and below.

Cautiously he edged back out onto open ground, narrowing his eyes. Was that a conversation he could hear in the distance? Creeping closer to the rim on the other side of the ridge, he took off his hat and peered over.

It was.

He strained hard, but he was too far away to make out what was being said.

For a moment he considered trying to move in closer. Certainly there was plenty of vegetation to hide him. Trouble was, there was a whole bunch of them down there; and it would only take one man with decent eyesight to spot him.

Stretching out flat on his belly, he brought the field-glasses up to his face. He had the sun behind him now, so he didn't have to worry about it bouncing off the lenses. The binoculars brought the riders a couple of hundred feet below into sharp relief. There were six . . . seven . . . ten of them in all.

He recognized Sobey first, then Fred. Moving the glasses a fraction more, he mouthed an unsociable word at the image of Charlie Kingold.

So the sonofabitch *had* decided to come after them!

But right now the marshal was having some kind of heated discussion with another man who was facing him and thus had his back to O'Brien. The fellow was dressed in a plain white shirt and black pants, with a brown leather gunbelt strapped high around his waist. He sat a sleek, well-fed dun and gestured frequently with the hand not holding the horse's reins.

O'Brien thought there was something familiar about him.

He wished he could get nearer to hear what they were saying. He'd have dearly loved to know what was going on. It looked very much like a falling out among thieves, but from this distance there was no clear way to tell.

Then the man with his back to O'Brien turned slightly and the soldier of fortune hurried to concentrate his magnified vision on the suddenly-revealed clear-cut and aristocratic profile.

The strange prophecy of He Who Sees came back to him in a rush. *In the next few days you will learn much of life and much of death. You must beware of a man wearing a blue bandanna, for he means you harm. And you must expect treachery — from one of the long-knives. An officer, for I see stripes on his sleeves.*

Well, he'd seen something of life during Owl Eye Woman's labor yesterday. And Kingold — the man with the blue bandanna — certainly meant him harm. And as for the treachery of an army officer?

Oh boy, he thought. He Who Sees had called it right all the way along.

Because he was looking at the officer in question right now.

It was General Crook's aide-de-camp.

Second Lieutenant William God-Damn Blevins.

Owl Eye Woman was strung out pretty tight by the time he got back. As soon as she saw him, she broke cover and hurried forward to ask, 'Well? What — ?'

He didn't need to answer her questions with words. Just hustling straight over to the horses and readying them to move out was answer enough.

182

The baby was sleeping on the blanket beneath the rock, its wrinkled face serene and innocent, so the squaw followed him over and offered to help. As he took his handgun back he said, 'Keep an eye on that ridge while I get these ribbons sorted out. Tell me the minute you see anyone top it.'

She nodded, her wide, coppery face a mask of apprehension. 'It is bad, then?'

'It could be better, sure.'

Somehow they got everything ready to move out inside fifteen minutes, during which time Owl Eye Woman reported no movement from the ridge, nor any signs of life anyplace else in the immediate vicinity.

'All right,' he said at last. 'Get up there on the seat.'

She did, slowly and obviously still sore. O'Brien climbed up beside her, took the reins and slapped them across the horses' backs. In her arms, the baby stirred briefly, fingers splayed, almost pitifully unaware of their danger.

They moved creakily up the slope,

following the narrow stream higher, the horses leaning into their leathers. O'Brien glanced across his shoulder. Still their back-trail appeared empty.

He couldn't shake the feeling that they would be spotted at any moment, though. A shout, a volley of gunfire, a chase they could not hope to win. It all seemed too real *not* to happen.

Then they began to pick up speed, and he twisted around to face front again, realizing that they had reached the top of the slope and would soon be lost beyond the ragged fold of land.

He did not spare the horses now, as the wagon rattled and bounced down into the tortured land below. He daren't. All the jogging back and forth woke the baby and it began to cry. But still he kept the pace merciless, glancing frequently over his shoulder.

The morning passed without incident or pursuit. The afternoon did likewise. But O'Brien did not relax his vigilance. He couldn't. So the buckboard continued rolling across all-but-impassable terrain at bone-shaking speed, chewing up miles just about as thoroughly as it chewed up man, woman and child.

There was no shade in which to grab five minutes' respite from the heat. The sun just kept up its yellow-white stare, squeezing them dry. The baby cried itself to sleep, awoke and cried some more. Owl Eye Woman rubbed at her sore back and stomach but voiced no complaint. And still O'Brien's red-rimmed eyes kept turning to their back-trail.

No-one came after them.

Only when they could go no further did he slow the killing pace. It was late afternoon, early evening, and their morning campsite now lay maybe as many as eighteen miles behind them.

They made cold-camp. The woman fed her baby, then tried to get some sleep. O'Brien, sitting with his back against a wagon wheel and the Winchester resting across his lap, watched the gradually-darkening wilderness through stinging eyes, allowing his thoughts to wander.

He wondered about Blevins and Kingold. How had they come to join forces? And why? And where was Manatee while all this was going on?

He sighed tiredly. There was something else, too. Something that bothered him more than anything else. Why hadn't there been any pursuit? Or, to put it another way, why hadn't there been any pursuit that he could *see*?

Sun-up next morning.

O'Brien came awake to the sound of Owl Eye Woman crying. Turning his head, he saw her through shadowy wheel-spokes, sitting cross-legged with the baby clasped to her, rocking back and forth. He watched the child reach out one small hand, touch her arm, yawn. It gave a contented gurgle. In its small, trusting world, everything was well. The squaw, however, knew different.

He lay there a moment longer, wishing he could do something to dispel the woman's sense of hopelessness. He knew exactly what she must be thinking; that she would never get to see her husband again, that he would never get to see his son. That mother and baby would end up cold and dead long before Cañon Calavera ever came into sight.

He made a big show of rolling out of his blankets, just to give her a chance to compose herself, and sure enough, by the time he'd come around to greet her, her cheeks were dry and her manner, while solemn, was not as openly despondent as it had been.

She had made a small fire, and now poured him a mug of coffee. He accepted it with a nod of thanks, hunkering beside her. 'How's the baby?' he asked gently.

She glanced at him, then away across the badlands, looking tired and drawn. 'He is well,' she replied. 'Considering.'

'And you?'

Her shoulders rose and fell in a shrug. 'The same.'

He sipped the coffee. It tasted bitter. 'You would like for me to cook you some food?' she asked.

He shook his head. 'No, thanks. We'll eat cold rations once we're on the move.'

But there was no further sign of pursuit from Blevins and Kingold that day, which was just as well, for the trail now became so bumpy and rock-littered that most of O'Brien's time was spent simply trying to negotiate all the obstacles in their path.

Sundown found them by another *tinaja*, only a pitiful seven or eight miles nearer their destination.

The following day was better. The land flattened out some and greened-up, too, so progress became easier, almost effortless, and that knowledge bolstered their badly-flagging spirits. When they camped that night and O'Brien consulted a somewhat dog-eared map he'd been given by Agent Smollett back in San Carlos, he estimated that Cañon Calavera lay no more than forty miles away — practically near enough to touch.

The next day — their seventh on the trail — began well. By the time the sun rose behind them they were already two miles from their campsite. Around midday, however, they ran into problems.

Topping a gentle incline, O'Brien brought the buckboard to a sudden halt to survey the land ahead through gritty, bloodshot eyes. Rolling sand-dunes spilled before them as far as the eye could see — and that meant trouble. He panned his gaze from left to right, hoping to spot an easy way around the loose, treacherous, bone-dry country ahead, but found none.

'*Senor?*'

He turned to face the woman.

'There is something wrong?' she asked.

He shook his head and said, 'No,' just to keep her from worrying. 'But I think we'll take this stretch nice 'n' easy, just to be on the safe side.'

He returned his stare to the shimmering, silk-smooth dunes one more time, then sighed and clucked the horses forward and down the slope. Almost immediately they ran into trouble, slipping to right and left as the wagon wheels sank deep in the free sand and turned only with effort.

O'Brien braced himself and urged the horses on, but their speed slowed alarmingly. The animals were finding it difficult to gain decent footing on the shifting sand, and were starting to stagger and panic.

Before long O'Brien passed the reins over to the woman and climbed down so that he could walk up front to guide and encourage them more effectively. About forty-five minutes later, the first of the dunes lay behind them — but another one stretched smooth and tan ahead.

They practically crawled along, continuing to slip and slide, often nearly losing control altogether. But through sheer persistence they made it across the second of the rolling hills — only to be confronted by a third.

When that one lay behind them they were exhausted. The sky was cloudless, the sun fierce, the trail they were leaving behind them so clear that even a blind man could follow it. But O'Brien summoned a crooked, sand-streaked smile of encouragement for Owl Eye Woman as he passed her a canteen of water, and she managed to find one for him, too.

He wiped a hand across his face, longing for a decent beer and a tub full of suds, then started back to the horses.

And that was when he heard it. Or rather, when he *didn't* hear it.

Seeing him halt and peer around, the squaw leaned forward on the seat to ask, 'What is it, *senor?* What is wrong?'

The desert was absolutely still. Not even the faintest of breezes blew up to stir the sand at his feet. He checked their back-trail. Nothing. Their left, their right. Nothing. Then he stared directly ahead, and his shoulders slumped.

'What is it?' she asked again, more

anxiously this time.

'Twister,' he said.

'What?'

'Dust-twister,' he replied, turning back to her. 'A sandstorm!'

She saw it for herself then, a faint yellow-brown wall of sand heading toward them at a steam-train's pace, still half a mile away but blowing closer all the time.

'Get down off there!' he snapped, breaking through the fear that held her captive on the seat. 'Quickly!'

She did as he commanded, feeling helpless and hopeless as he began to unhitch the team-horses in a series of sharp, desperate fumblings.

'Get some rags out of the back of the wagon,' he said without looking up. 'Tie one across your nose and mouth and do the same for the baby.'

'*Si!*'

'And fetch me some rope! I'm gonna have to fix up some hobbles for these horses to make sure they don't bolt when that duster hits!'

Later she would wonder how he managed to do all that he did in so short a time. As she hugged the wailing child close to her breast, it seemed that he worked with the strength and speed of a god. He fashioned hobbles for all three horses, then went around to the far side of the buckboard and, gritting his teeth, began to lift it. She saw what he was trying to do almost at once. There was no cover behind which they could hide, so he was trying to make some. But he could not lift the wagon high enough to push it onto its side, especially with his injured left arm.

Again and again he tried, teeth clenched and muscles bulging, only to fail. In the end he couldn't spare any more time, because the sandstorm was almost upon them.

'All right, get underneath!' he yelled to make himself heard above the terrifying roar.

She did, trying to placate the frightened baby as she went.

O'Brien waited until she was out of

sight, checked to make sure the brake was on, then tied the animals' reins to the nearest wheel. He slid beneath the wagon just as flying sand began to sting their hands and faces. 'Here,' he shouted, draping a blanket over the woman and child. 'Don't worry. Everything will be all right. Just stay put and try not to panic!'

He didn't hear her reply; it was lost in the storm's banshee howl.

They huddled face-down beneath the wagon, hardly daring to breathe the warm, stifling air. O'Brien thought he heard the whinny and stamp of the horses, then a particularly shrill cry from the four-day-old baby, but in all the chaos he might only have imagined it.

Above them the wagon gave a threatening creak, buffeted by cyclonic winds. Buried in the dark, uncertain world behind their closed eyelids, the man and the squaw fought hard to stay calm and sit it out. But instead of abating, the storm seemed to intensify.

They waited fretfully, hoping, always hoping, that it would end. But the duster raged on. O'Brien chanced a turn of the head and found the woman watching him. Above them the horses tugged at their restraining bonds; the wagon creaked again, shifting ever so slightly; the baby loosed a pitiful sob. The squaw trembled, reaching out to fix one small brown hand tightly on his wrist.

An entire hour passed, or was it only ten slow minutes? Neither of them could tell, for time lost all meaning. But gradually the wind lessened and the stinging sand began to ease up.

When silence finally returned to the dunes they were almost too deafened to hear it. Slowly O'Brien lifted his head to look around. Sand trickled from his hat-brim and shoulders. Without a word he crawled out from beneath the partially-buried wagon and got to his feet, using his hat to beat the dust off his crumpled clothes.

He coughed, grabbed a canteen of

water, passed it down to the still-shocked woman and went to check on the horses. He ran his hands across them, muttering nonsense as he checked their eyes and legs. Save for a bad case of nerves and several small cuts where sharp particles of sand had sliced their exposed flesh, they were all right.

Behind him, Owl Eye Woman slithered out from beneath the wagon, the baby quiet now, and full of wonder at the sudden silence.

'You all right?' he asked.

She cleared her throat, put one hand to her smudged forehead. 'Yes.'

She passed him the canteen and he tilted his head back to drink. The water was warm but felt good on his scratchy throat. He drank deep, losing himself for a moment, until Owl Eye Woman suddenly cried out.

In an instant he released his hold on the canteen and reached for the Lightning on his hip. 'What is it?' he snapped.

'Th — there,' she breathed, pointing ahead of them. 'Advancing upon us! R-riders!'

7

With an oath O'Brien hauled his Winchester from its sheath and jacked a shell into the breech.

'Owl Eye Woman, get around here!'

By the time she was standing next to him behind the pathetic cover of the buckboard, he had propped the long gun against a wagon wheel and taken out his field-glasses. She watched as he brought them up to his face.

Now he could see the approaching riders clearer through the dancing, super-hot air. There were five of them, about a quarter of a mile out, pushing their mounts as fast as they could across the uncooperative terrain.

Another curse spilled from his lips. No wonder there hadn't been any pursuit from behind — the sonsof-bitches had swung around to intercept them from up *ahead*, and just like a

Judas goat O'Brien had led the woman he'd been hired to protect right into their clutches!

But wait . . .

He stiffened. These riders, they were wearing army blues. They were *soldiers!* And the officer in the lead —

O'Brien nearly loosed a rebel yell when he recognized the round, rugged face of Corporal Robinson.

He swung around to face the squaw, setting the glasses aside. 'It's all right, Owl Eye Woman! They're soldiers!'

Her eyebrows lowered in a frown. '*What?*'

'The officer out front, he's the adjutant at Fort Bisbee. General Crook must've sent him out to meet us.'

Understanding suddenly showed in her eyes. 'Then . . . it is over? The running?'

'As good as.'

Her eyes filled with tears. 'Oh, *senor* — '

She came into his arms naturally, without thought, her and her baby; and

O'Brien held them both as the woman struggled to compose herself before their saviors arrived.

Sometime between five and ten minutes later, Corporal Robinson and his four men rode up, all of them dusty and red-faced. The young adjutant smiled down at them and nodded a greeting. 'Mr. O'Brien! I was hoping we'd run into you!'

'Well, I can't tell you how much we hoped we'd run into *you*, Robinson.'

The corporal's eyes travelled to the Apache woman. 'This is Coyote's wife?' he asked.

O'Brien nodded. 'Yep. And the little feller in her arms is an addition we picked up somewhere along the way. I guess you could call him Coyote Junior.'

Robinson chuckled. 'Well, well, well.'

Then he brought out a long-barreled Cavalry Colt and stuck it right in their faces.

Owl Eye Woman cried out, stiffening. O'Brien took a pace forward to put himself in front of her.

'That's far enough, O'Brien!' Robinson snapped. 'I mean it! Don't even blink or I'll fire!'

O'Brien did as he was told, looking at the men behind the corporal for the first time, seeing big, rough hellions in ill-fitting uniforms, with hard, soulless faces and arctic eyes. *Soldiers?* No. Men in soldiers' *uniforms;* not quite the same thing.

He felt sick.

'Good,' Robinson went on, somewhat calmer, 'Now, reach across with your left hand and take out that sidearm. Fingertips only, O'Brien, no fancy stuff! That's it. Now toss it over there. Good.'

O'Brien's face was flushed with anger. 'I don't get it, Robinson. What's this all about?'

'Oh come now, Mr. O'Brien. I know that you're a fairly simple soul, brawn before brains and all that, but even *you* can't be that naïve.'

The blue-eyed soldier of fortune shook his head, somehow finding the gall to smile unpleasantly up at his captor. 'No,' he said quietly. 'No, I don't suppose I am.'

He stepped back to the cowering squaw and put an arm around her shoulders, ostensibly to comfort her but in reality preparing to shove her to the sand at the same time he went for the rifle propped against the wagon wheel.

'You were behind those attempts on my life just before I reached Bisbee,' he said, playing for time.

'*And* the one just after you and Panayatishn left for San Carlos,' the corporal replied.

'Figures. I knew someone on the General's staff was to blame. Who else knew where to find me? But hell, were you really that leery of my reputation to go to all that trouble?'

'Yes,' Robinson replied candidly. 'You see, I reached pretty much the same conclusion as General Crook — that if for some reason Jim Sundance, his usual 'hired gun', couldn't handle this mission, only one other man could

— the fearsome Carter O'Brien.'

'So you tried to stop me from taking it by sending Manatee after me.'

'Manatee and a few of his men, yes. But I guess everything I heard about you was true. Despite all the odds, you got through. I salute you.'

O'Brien narrowed his eyes. 'Who is Manatee, anyway?'

'My, my, such curiosity, Mr. O'Brien!'

'Well, let's just say that I'd hate to die in ignorance.'

'Very well,' Robinson said with a laugh. 'Manatee is my . . . partner in this venture.'

'What venture?'

'That's enough questions, I think.'

But O'Brien pursued it. 'What is it you're after, Robinson? What can you gain by keeping this Apache war going? Promotion?'

The corporal shrugged. 'Well, it *is* true that nothing improves a fellow's chances of climbing up the ranks quite so much as an opportunity to prove himself in battle. But there are

. . . other considerations.'

'Like money for the sale of guns to the Indians?'

'*Gold*,' Robinson corrected, the word stirring something nasty in his otherwise pleasant brown eyes. 'Apache gold, Mr. O'Brien, a veritable fortune of it. And why shouldn't I benefit from a war with heathens like Coyote? As adjutant at Fort Bisbee, I am in the perfect position to appropriate weapons and ammunition for resale through Manatee's good offices. He is happy, I am happy, the Indians are happy.'

'It's an ill wind,' said O'Brien.

'Exactly.'

The fighting-man swallowed hard. He didn't much relish the prospect, but the time had come to ask the bottom-line question. 'What happens now?' he said. 'To the woman, I mean.'

The smile on Robinson's countenance was cold and reptilian. 'Nothing — yet. She has an appointment to keep with her husband.' His smile grew wider. 'And what more provocation will

Coyote need to spark off a full-scale uprising than to see U.S. troopers — ' he indicated the four men with him ' — gun down his precious bride and son right before his eyes?'

O'Brien tensed himself, preparing to grab the Winchester. 'You're crazy,' he muttered with disgust.

Robinson shrugged. 'No. Just ambitious. Now, hands up, O'Brien. I don't want to have to kill you yet. After all, we're going to need someone expendable to drive this sorry-looking buckboard into Cañon Calavera for us. But if you try anything foolish . . . '

O'Brien hesitated, running his eyes across the five guns trained on him. The urge to strike back was almost beyond control. But maybe this wasn't the right time. Perhaps if he went quietly, lulled them into a false sense of security . . .

Grimly he raised his hands.

The corporal's troopers — almost certainly some of Manatee's men in stolen uniforms — were good. In next to no time they had him tightly bound and shoved in back of the wagon, with Owl Eye Woman studying him through glazed, uncomprehending eyes.

'Now,' said Robinson with a tug at one of his impressive side-whiskers. The team had been re-hitched and some of the accumulated sand shoveled away from the wheels. 'We have two appointments to keep — firstly with Manatee and the rest of the men, and then with the notorious Coyote himself. Looking forward to them, are you, Mr. O'Brien?'

O'Brien told him to do something both acrobatic and intensely painful, but Robinson only laughed. Then they moved out.

Just beyond the dunes the land firmed up and began to rise and fall in an apparently endless series of yucca-dotted hills. O'Brien watched the country without much interest, still trying to sift all the implications of what Corporal Robinson had told him through his mind.

At about four o'clock both he and Owl Eye Woman sensed a stirring of excitement up ahead and managed to peer around the hard case assigned wagon-duty to see green mountain slopes lifting away to either side of a shadowy canyon entrance about a hundred yards further down the trail.

As the horses' hooves clattered back off the high stone walls, he and the squaw traded stares. She was scared bad, and with good reason. Hell, he was scared himself, if it came to that.

When the wagon and its small escort came to a halt, the captives found themselves in a long, narrow box canyon. To their right O'Brien spotted a makeshift corral housing approximately twelve unsaddled horses. Closer was a large campfire around which five or six men were eating stew and drinking coffee. O'Brien shifted his gaze, counted three rifle-toting guards at the canyon entrance, another few either dozing or playing cards on the other side of the coulee.

Twelve men, he thought, weighing the odds. Twelve men plus Robinson and the four he'd brought with him. Seventeen guns . . .

Roughly he and the squaw were bundled out of the wagon and onto their knees. Most of the men — who had been dragged from the same slimy underbelly as the bogus soldiers — came to form a curious circle around them. A few laughed and pointed when the baby started to cry. A few more stared lustfully at the woman's bare legs. A shadow fell across O'Brien. He heard a voice say, 'So this is him.' He looked up.

Manatee returned his scrutiny.

'So you're the high and mighty Carter O'Brien,' he said.

O'Brien didn't reply. But Manatee was exactly as He Who Sees had described him. He stood roughly five and a half feet in height and was of slim build. His face was long and narrow, and weathered by thirty-five summers. His hair was shoulder-length and fair; brow heavy and menacing; eyes gray-green and cold. He wore a checked cotton shirt, California pants, high-heeled boots, a flat-crowned, broad-brimmed hat.

But even the big Smith & Wesson American riding at his hip failed to make him stand out. He was, as the Apache shaman had said, insignificant, a nobody. But that was his strength, O'Brien realized. Manatee could come and go as he pleased, anywhere in the country, and no-one would ever give him a second glance.

'I told you we could take him easier if he thought he was going to get some help from the army,' Robinson said with a laugh.

'Well done,' Manatee replied. To the bogus soldiers he said, 'Go get some coffee, boys. Evans, Doyle! Move these three across to that jumble of rocks yonder. Doyle, you keep watch on 'em. Evans, relieve him in two hours.'

They were half-dragged, half-pushed to the area Manatee had specified, and all but thrown into the dirt. The buckboard was wheeled away, the animals unhitched. The men went back to their various pursuits and silence descended upon their hideout once again.

O'Brien closed his eyes, clenched his teeth and strained at the ropes holding his arms behind his back. But he already knew that they'd been tied by an expert; he could feel every complicated knot digging into his wrists.

'You . . . you are all right, *senor?*'

He opened his eyes to see Owl Eye Woman's beautiful but tear-streaked face watching him. Even her baby's large brown eyes seemed to be focused on him.

'Yeah, sure.'

But he couldn't hide the pain in his eyes as he looked at the squaw and her baby.

Robinson's plan to kill them both right in front of Coyote could only have sprung from a diseased mind; the very thought of it made him re-double his efforts to break free until —

'*Hey!*'

Almost before he knew it, O'Brien found himself looking down the barrel of a Henry repeater being held by Doyle, the dark-skinned man who had been ordered to guard them.

'You keep that up an' I'm gonna have to give you a hole where you don't want one,' the hard case warned laconically.

O'Brien lay back with a sigh, trying to come up with some other means of escape. Behind him high walls rose skyward with nary a hand-hold. Ahead stretched only coverless canyon floor. No matter which way he viewed it, there was only one way in and one way out — and the way out was well guarded.

Damn. Maybe he should've made a fight of it back at the dunes after all.

The woman was still looking at him, seeking comfort. He wanted to reassure her, tell her not to worry, that everything would pan out okay, but how could he when he couldn't even reassure himself?

'*Lo siento*,' he said in a whisper. 'I'm sorry.'

'Settling in, O'Brien?'

He turned again as Robinson came over, steam rising from the enamel mug in his hand. Behind him, Manatee and his men laughed and joked or slept to pass the time.

'Good, good,' the corporal continued. 'I thought I'd just let you know that we'll be moving out at first light tomorrow. We're only about twenty-some miles from Cañon Calavera now, so we should reach it comfortably around this time tomorrow afternoon.'

O'Brien made an unpleasant sound in his throat. 'At the risk of sounding *naive* again,' he said with heavy sarcasm, 'shouldn't you be pushing a pen back at Fort Bisbee right now? I mean, won't you be missed?'

Robinson drank from his mug, then toyed with his reddish-brown side-whiskers again. 'Even a lowly corporal is allowed leave of absence every now and then,' he replied smugly. 'As far as my superiors back at base are concerned, I am on a three-day furlough in Sierra Vista right now.'

'Looks like you've thought of everything,' O'Brien said mildly, adding mentally, *you smart-ass bastard.*

The corporal lifted one shoulder modestly. 'I try to.'

He left them alone then; they all did, as the sun sank lower and the box canyon grew dark save for the orange glow of the campfire. A bottle or two came out as evening wore on. O'Brien watched the hard, fire-reddened faces of the gunrunners as they took long, greedy swallows of the acidic bust-head. Beside him, Owl Eye Woman rocked back and forth, back and forth, trying to comfort herself as much as the child.

There had to be a way out of this, he told himself. There *must* be. But what was it? *Think, man, think!*

All he got for his pains was a headache.

Somehow he managed to doze, wake, doze again, as did the squaw. The night passed slowly, and with a bitter chill. When the sun rose again it found the captives hollow-eyed and sluggish.

But Robinson was as good as his word; even before the long gray streaks of false dawn had properly left the sky, the men were saddled up and ready to ride.

As they were shoved back over to the buckboard, O'Brien sensed an almost unholy feeling of anticipation among their captors. They were actually looking forward to Owl Eye Woman's murder, because by that act each of them stood to make a fortune. The realization soured his guts.

Manatee joined the corporal at the head of the long, raggle-tail line; then came the wagon, with O'Brien and Owl Eye Woman in back; then the rest of the men, including the four bogus troopers.

The sun rose fast, warming the land quickly to furnace heat. O'Brien's arms had gone to sleep. Now he rolled onto his side and got the squaw to rub them as the miles unwound beneath them. It took some time, but once he could feel his fingertips tingling he kept his hands moving without further assistance, doggedly forcing circulation back into them.

Eight o'clock . . . nine . . . nine-thirty . . . ten . . .

Three miles . . . five miles . . . eight miles . . .

O'Brien stared up at the wide blue sky, ignoring the clatter and creak of the wagon, the regular clip-clop of horse-hooves, the muted chatter of the men. *Just wait 'til they untie me*, he thought. *That's all, I'll — I'll what?*

What *could* he do against seventeen men? Not much, without help. But maybe he'd find a little help. His rifle, perhaps, or —

Ten-thirty . . . eleven . . .

Fifteen miles . . . sixteen . . . eighteen . . .

'*Whoa!*'

The buckboard came to a sudden, jolting halt, stirring him from his heat-induced reverie. Looking around, he saw that the column had stopped in a dry wash about fifteen feet wide and maybe four or five hundred yards to the first lazy bend. Bright yellow needle-grass grew thickly along both sloping banks, as did garambullo cactus and orange caltrop flowers.

There was much activity now, as O'Brien struggled to sit upright. The men were dismounting and loosening cinches. A couple started gathering fuel for a fire, while another broke out a large tin of Arbuckle coffee.

O'Brien glanced up at the sun; it was about one o'clock.

'Get them down offa there!' Manatee barked, walking his dapple grey past the wagon.

Immediately a thick-set man with a flowing black beard hurried to do his bidding, pulling O'Brien off the wagon-bed to land hard on his butt and taking a more intimate hold of Owl Eye Woman.

'And untie O'Brien,' Robinson added, striding up.

O'Brien looked at him and the corporal smiled.

'Yes,' he said in reply to the fighting-man's unspoken question. 'We're only about six miles east of Cañon Calavera now. Once the rest of us have had a breather, it'll be time for you to drive the squaw here to her destiny.'

As O'Brien got to his feet the big man with the beard used a sharp knife to slice through the ropes, then walked away, leaving him to pull what was left of the hemp from his chafed wrists.

'How are you going to work it?' O'Brien asked in a dry, gravelly voice as the corporal beat dust from his fatigue blouse with a pair of white gloves. 'Just out of interest?'

'Simple,' Robinson replied, watching Manatee move among his men, who had congregated about thirty feet away, pointing here, issuing an order there. 'My four 'troopers' and I will escort you to within sight of Cañon Calavera, then let you go. You will whip up your team and we will give chase. All the noise will attract Coyote, who will appear just in time to see us kill the three of you.'

O'Brien flexed his fingers. 'You're taking an awful lot for granted, Robinson. Suppose we manage to out-run you? Get into Cañon Calavera before — '

'You won't,' the corporal interrupted. 'I chose Manatee's finest shots for this stage of the game. You'll be killed at exactly the right moment, I promise you.'

O'Brien worked up some saliva and spat. 'Thanks,' he said quietly. 'You're all heart.'

Robinson strode off.

'What . . . what are they . . . ?' Owl Eye Woman's Spanish was halting now, as fear made it hard for her to concentrate on her second language. 'It is bad, *si?*'

He nodded. '*Si.*'

He didn't look at her because he was too busy scanning both ends of the dry wash, desperately trying to come up with a plan of escape. But what chance

218

was there against seventeen guns?

'Aaaah!'

He spun around just as Owl Eye Woman pushed one of Manatee's men away from her. He was a big fellow with tobacco-brown skin, forty years old and bald as a coot. O'Brien had noticed him watching the squaw last night — he had the look of a one-time sailor about him.

'Ah, come on, don't be like that — '

Owl Eye Woman said something to him in Apache, but his only response was a grin — a lustful grin. Again he approached her, calloused hands outstretched.

'Ah, come on now, all I want's a little feel o' what you got beneath that buckskin dress!'

But before he could make another grab for her, O'Brien lashed out with a haymaker that sent him flopping back into the dust.

A few of the other men, having seen what happened, laughed.

'Why you scurvy son of a sidewinder, you'll pay for that!'

The sea-dog regained his feet quickly, hauling a curved blade from a sheath on his thick leather belt.

Seeing it, O'Brien planted himself more firmly in front of the squaw, preparing himself for the other man's attack. But before the fight could begin, two things happened.

A gunshot rang out — and a bullet tore messily through the bald man's head.

8

Owl Eye Woman screamed. The baby started wailing. But even before the sea-dog fell dead and quivering at their feet, all eyes had turned to the figure standing high on the arroyo's south bank.

'Hold it, the lot of you!' shouted Second Lieutenant William Blevins, jacking another shell into the Winchester he held trained on the gunrunners.

Doyle, the man with the repeater, however, must have been deaf. He made a move for his gun and Blevins fired again.

The slug threw Doyle back against the far bank and tore a scream from him as he bounced off to land in the dust, clutching a ruined right shoulder.

'*Tell* them, Manatee!' the lieutenant snapped. 'One wrong move and you get the next bullet!'

O'Brien saw blood drain from Manatee's long face as he stared down Blevins' rifle barrel. On the ground, the bald man stopped quivering and lay still, bleeding heavily into the thirsty earth.

Still confused, O'Brien bent and pulled a Remington Army .44 from the dead man's belt, then thumbed back the hammer.

'All right, you heard 'im!' Manatee croaked, raising his hands. 'Do whatever he says.'

'That's more like it,' said Blevins. 'Now, the rest of you, do like your boss and raise your hands. That's it. Get down on your bellies, all of you. You too, Robinson.'

At the sound of his name, the round-faced corporal shook off his surprise. 'Ah . . . Blevins! Thank God you've arrived! I — '

'Spare me any more of your lies, corporal. I know you're up to your ears in this; we've long suspected your involvement in a number of other shady deals, too. So get down on your stomach like the others!'

Robinson did, slowly and with much muttering.

The lieutenant was dressed as he had been the day O'Brien spied him in conference with Charlie Kingold — white shirt, black pants, grey hat. Now, without taking his eyes off the gunrunners, he said, 'Are you and the woman all right, O'Brien?'

'Yeah. But what — ?'

'No time for explanations now. Let's just say that General Crook stuck me on your tail as a little extra insurance, just to make sure you reached Cañon Calavera in one piece.'

He came down the slope to join O'Brien then, still keeping his rifle on the horizontal low-lives.

'You mean you've been following me ever since I left Fort Bisbee?' O'Brien asked, stunned.

'Yes.'

'Then that business with the Wildcat sheriff — '

' — was me threatening him with military prosecution if he continued to come after you,' the lieutenant finished. 'Now, do you think we could delay any further questions for a while? This is neither the time nor the place, as I'm sure you must agree.'

'I reckon.'

'Good. Then get back in that wagon and head straight for Cañon Calavera at once.'

O'Brien stiffened. 'What about these *hombres?*'

A grim smile tugged at Blevins' thin lips. 'What about them? You're not suggesting we *arrest* them, are you?'

'No, but — '

'Then I'll hold them back for as long as I can.'

O'Brien shook his head. 'Uh-huh. I reckon I owe you one, Blevins. Me and the woman both. That's why we're all getting out of here together.'

'Now see here — '

'Look, just quit arguing and cover me while I get my horse, will you?'

Without waiting for a reply, O'Brien carefully edged around the prone gunrunners and cut out his appaloosa from the other nervy mounts. He walked the animal back to the buckboard and mounted up, slipping his own Winchester from its sheath.

'Help the woman into the wagon and get up there on the seat, lieutenant,' he said, keeping his restless blue eyes on Manatee and the others. 'Then start the team toward that bend up yonder. I'll cover you as long as I can, then catch up with you out on open range.'

Blevins opened his mouth to protest, but O'Brien's attention was elsewhere. From the corner of his eye he'd seen a small-boned Mexican about twenty feet away slowly move his left hand towards the butt of a Le Mat. Just as his fingers closed around it, O'Brien sent a .44/.40 bullet into the ground ahead of him, spraying a fountain of dirt over the fellow's black hair.

'Next one tries that buys himself a one-way ticket to hell!' he growled.

No-one tried it. No-one fancied making the trip.

While O'Brien kept them covered, Blevins helped the woman into the wagon and went up front, winding the reins around his smooth hands. It was plain that he didn't like the idea of leaving O'Brien to it, but there was no time to stand around and debate the point. The safe delivery of Owl Eye Woman was of paramount importance.

The lieutenant kicked off the brake and O'Brien heard the wagon begin to rattle away behind him.

'*Damn you, Blevins!*' It was Robinson, his round face crimson with fury. '*You too, O'Brien! I'll —* '

'Shuddup,' said Manatee, calm as death.

'Yeah — and keep kissing dirt, the lot of you,' O'Brien growled.

Behind him, the now-familiar wagon sounds were growing still fainter. With luck, Owl Eye Woman would soon be on the final leg of her journey, and from her new home up in the Sierra Madres all this would be remembered as little more than a passing nightmare.

'What are you going to do with us?' Robinson demanded indignantly. 'What can you do against *all* of us?'

O'Brien's smile was bleak. 'Let's just hope you don't have to find out,' he replied.

'He's got a point, though,' Manatee said in that same dangerous tone. 'You can't keep us belly-down like this forever, O'Brien. If one of us doesn't manage to get the drop on you now, you can bet we'll come after you the minute you light out to join up with that stinkin' squaw.'

It was defiant talk, the kind Manatee's men wanted to hear. An ominous rumble went through them, and O'Brien had a nasty feeling they were getting ready to launch some kind of retaliatory action. But if the sounds still reaching him from behind were anything to go by, at least the wagon had almost disappeared from sight.

'You'll come after me, will you?' he

asked conversationally, as if he wasn't feeling sore and tired and hungry at all. 'Hell, I'd like to see that, Manatee. But I think I'd better warn you that you'll be doing it without horses.'

'What?'

'I'll be running yours off just before I leave here.'

One of the other men, a thirty-year-old red-head with a lumpy face, looked up. 'Hey now, mister, don't tell me you'd leave us all a-foot out here in the middle o' nowhere!'

'I just did,' O'Brien replied harshly. 'And while I'm at it, I'll tell you something else, too. You're not going to get away with this, any of you. Because as soon as I've seen Owl Eye Woman safely on her way, I'll be back, and no matter where you run, I'll find you.'

'Sonofabitch,' Manatee said in defeat.

Then he yelled, 'Now!' and Evans, the hard case next to him, rolled over and came up with a fistful of Colt.

His bullet blasted through the heavy afternoon air and struck the arroyo bank just above O'Brien's head, sending a shower of rock chips across his shoulders.

The appaloosa shied and side-stepped beneath him. He had a brief, blurred vision of the gunrunners rising to their feet and pulling iron. Instinctively he fired the Winchester, pumped the action, fired again. Evans screamed, fell back into his friends with his face full of blood.

For two heart-stopping seconds there was nothing but confusion. Then the horse completed its turn and took off at a gallop along the dry wash, following the buckboard tracks for all it was worth.

O'Brien heard more gunfire as he bent low across the animal's straining neck. Gunfire; shouting; his own rasping breath loud in his ears.

Suddenly the hot air was crowded with lead. He kicked his heels into the horse's barrel. For another ten seconds he knew only the pounding of the animal's hooves against rock. Then the appaloosa followed the lazy bend up and out of the dry wash, and O'Brien tried to figure how long it would take the gunrunners to organize pursuit. They would have to calm their skittish mounts, tighten cinches. They might take their time rounding the arroyo bend and coming up onto open range, just in case O'Brien had decided to wait for them. But whichever way he looked at it, he only had minutes at best — perhaps only one minute.

He urged the horse to greater speed.

Up ahead, about half a mile away, he spotted the buckboard bouncing recklessly across the desert floor, the team animals leaning hard into the traces. From this distance, the wagon looked old and frail; for the first time O'Brien wondered whether or not it could withstand such punishment over this last half-dozen miles.

But then he heard another burst of gunfire behind him and hipped around in the heaving saddle to get a jarred view of Robinson, Manatee and their remaining men fairly thundering up and out of the dry wash after him.

He faced front again, narrowing his eyes against the rush of wind pushing at his face and sending his horse's mane flying in a wild tangle.

He'd caught up with the buckboard just a shade. As it sped hell for leather across the uneven terrain its wheels left the ground, spun, landed again with bone-breaking force. He found himself wondering about the woman in back of the wagon, hanging on for dear life as the desperate pace threw her and her baby around without mercy.

Another glance across his shoulder. How far back were the gunrunners now? A quarter-mile? Slightly more, he decided. They were riding stirrup to stirrup, fourteen of them, yelling like the very braves they'd been hoping to exploit.

Again O'Brien faced front.

'*Judas!*'

The appaloosa's path was blocked by a whole cluster of barrel cactus.

This is it, he thought. *I'm done for*.

But without breaking stride, the horse took the obstacle in a single bound. O'Brien lost his balance, regained it, clutched the reins in his free hand even tighter and wound them around his saddle horn for a firmer grip.

In those hectic minutes nothing registered with him save the regular tattoo of shod hooves and the occasional staccato burst of gunfire behind him.

How far had they come? Two miles, two and a half? Then Cañon Calavera was still about four miles away.

Damn!

But at last the buckboard was continuing to make good speed across the wilderness. He saw Blevins standing up now, long legs spread for balance as he lashed the reins across the team-horses' shining flanks. They might just make it y —

Suddenly O'Brien's appaloosa gave a cough, broke stride, stumbled, and with a sick feeling he knew the animal had stopped a bullet.

The appaloosa's forelegs went first, then it began to plough nose first into the dust. O'Brien kicked free of the stirrups about three seconds before he was thrown over the dying animal's head.

He hit the ground running, the Winchester still clutched in his fists, turned just as the horse crashed to the ground in a heap and scrambled back towards it.

The wheezing animal was bleeding from a wound in its left haunch and two of its legs had been broken in the fall. O'Brien stared down at the horse, devastated by its loss. But there was no time for mourning.

As dispassionately as he knew how, he aimed the rifle at its forehead, fired once, then flopped behind the dead creature and drew a bead on the advancing gunrunners.

You're going to pay now, he told himself grimly. *God, you're going to pay.*

They were closing the distance quickly. Their bullets were beginning to pepper the sage-dotted land around him. But O'Brien ignored them, pumping a fresh shell into the breech.

Slowly he brought the stock of the Winchester up to his right cheek and took aim. The calmness in him was frightening.

Closer . . . closer . . .

His finger whitened on the trigger. The rifle bucked and boomed. One of the hard cases spilled from his saddle, rolled, lay still.

O'Brien worked the lever again, shifting his aim. *Thirteen left*, he thought. *Unlucky for some.*

He fired. Missed. Bullets chopped the air around him. A couple slapped into the appaloosa's unfeeling hide.

The hard cases came nearer. O'Brien fired again. His next bullet struck one of the oncoming horses in the head. The creature went down as if pole-axed, spilling its rider to the ground, where he rolled and lay still.

The rest of them came on.

O'Brien drew another bead and fired; another, fired; one more. Two shots missed. The third one didn't. One of the bogus troopers clutched his suddenly-bloody chest, somersaulted from his saddle, landed on his head and died.

But there was no stopping them now that their blood was up. Still they came on, faster than ever, returning fire wildly from the backs of their galloping horses.

Manatee was in the lead. O'Brien rose to his feet just as the boss gunrunner reached his position. He fired from the hip, missed, up-ended the rifle to use it as a club and knocked the other man out of his saddle. Manatee flew backwards, hit the ground hard on his ass, gasped, rolled, came up fast with a gun in his hand.

But before he could use it, something incredible happened.

An arrow struck him right in the belly.

He didn't even have the chance to

register surprise. He tumbled back into the dirt already stiffening, as O'Brien — who had grown increasingly aware of a mixture of pounding hooves and war cries from behind him — spun around.

Twenty bronzed Apaches raced their horses past him to engage the rest of the gunrunners in combat. He sagged a little, half-fell behind the appaloosa to get his breath back. He felt weak, disoriented, not quite sure what was going on.

But the identity of the newcomers was plain enough — Coyote and his fellow renegades!

The noise was deafening as both sides joined in battle. Yells and shouts, whoops and screams, gunfire and the panicky shrieks of terrified horses all echoed across the rolling desert floor. O'Brien saw two more hard cases fall from their saddles, fairly bristling with arrows. Another hit the dirt with a hatchet in his face. A brave was shot; another horse fell mortally wounded.

The stench of blood hung on the air, mingling with the foul scent of death.

In the thick of the fray, Corporal Robinson shot a warrior in the stomach and watched him leave his horse guts-first.

The lieutenant had had his fill of this. Dealing with the Apaches was one thing — fighting them something else again.

As he yanked his horse around and made to retreat, what was left of Manatee's gang — a pitiful seven men — decided to follow his example, peeling away from the confrontation without further ceremony.

But O'Brien knew they wouldn't get far.

The Apaches didn't give chase. They didn't need to.

As the fleeing white men widened the gap between them, the renegades lined up facing them and nocked fresh arrows to their juniper bows.

Without any apparent rush, they brought the weapons up to aim, something almost ritualistic about their actions.

O'Brien held his breath, watching the gunrunners increase the range between them.

Still the Apaches made no move. Then —

They released their arrows in a sudden rush of air. O'Brien watched them fly high and fast, up, up, ever higher. Then they reached their highest point and began to descend, graceful but deadly.

He followed their course with morbid fascination.

The arrows came down on the fleeing whites like fatal rain and ran each man through in three or four different places.

O'Brien doubted that Robinson or the gunrunners ever knew what hit them.

As one they stiffened, screamed and fell dead or dying to the ground. Some were dragged by their horses, others just left to squirm in the sand, praying for a swift end to the pain.

Still slumped behind the dead appaloosa, O'Brien decided that he'd seen enough. He screwed his eyes tight to shut out the whole gory tableau and tried mightily to fight back the nausea that suddenly threatened to overtake him.

And that was how the Apaches found him when they came back fifteen minutes later.

Cañon Calavera; sundown.

Sitting with their backs to the canyon's high north wall, O'Brien and Blevins watched the Apaches preparing to embark on the first leg of their journey south.

They had been fed and watered, after a fashion, then left to rest and lick their wounds. Now the day was quiet and peaceful, although sunset had splashed more blood across the wide, empty sky to remind them of the afternoon's violence.

O'Brien turned to glance at the young lieutenant, echoing the other man's question. 'What am I going to do now?' he asked. 'Now that I've gone through my 'divorce', you mean?'

Blevins smiled.

'Well . . . first of all, I've got to collect my saddle-gear from . . . from where I left it,' O'Brien continued. 'And then I've got to see General Crook about my thousand dollars.'

Blevins nodded. 'And then?'

'And then,' O'Brien said with relish, 'I'm going home to Tombstone for a while — to sleep for about a month.'

He sat there a moment longer, enjoying the chill as evening freshened the gentle breeze, until Blevins gave him a nudge. O'Brien turned to him again. 'Looks like your squaw's just about ready to say goodbye,' the army officer said quietly.

O'Brien followed his gaze. Owl Eye Woman and Coyote had come to stand about twenty feet away. Behind them, Coyote's men were already aboard their horses, anxious to be making tracks at last. One of them cradled the little baby with surprising care.

O'Brien rose and strode across to them, tuckered as hell, his shadow thrown long across the golden canyon's sloping floor. Again he studied Coyote. The Apache didn't have the look of a killer. He was hardly much taller than his squaw, and his wide face, high cheekbones, flat nose and deep black eyes told nothing of his homicidal nature.

But his bare, muscular torso bore many scars, some new, some old and healed, and thus gave testimony to the many battles in which he'd taken part.

'My husband has neither Spanish nor English, senor,' Owl Eye Woman said apologetically. 'So he cannot thank you for himself. But he wants it to be known that you are a man of great honor, and that he will always be in your debt.'

O'Brien shrugged uncomfortably. He muttered something about Coyote's generosity but what he really meant was, 'Forget it.'

'Coyote has a gift he would like you to have,' she said, touching the renegade on the arm.

The Apache reached into a small pouch at his belt and brought out something soft which he offered to O'Brien. O'Brien took it before he properly knew what it was and said, '*Gracias*.' Then Coyote turned away.

A second later, his woman did likewise.

They mounted two spirited pintos and moved slowly to the head of their somewhat depleted column. Then, without a backward glance, they rode away.

O'Brien watched them go as the canyon gradually fell silent around him. He wasn't quite sure how he felt about never seeing the woman or her baby again. After a while, Lieutenant Blevins came across to stand beside him.

'Well?' the younger man asked briskly. 'What now? Make camp here and head back to Bisbee tomorrow, or leave now, before those aborigines decide to come back and add two more names to their list of victims?'

O'Brien turned to face him. 'Move out now,' he said, offering the officer Coyote's gift. 'Here, lieutenant. I've got no use for this; you might as well keep it as a souvenir.'

Blevins took it, genuinely surprised. 'Why — thank you.'

O'Brien took three steps toward the buckboard before the lieutenant gave a yelp. 'My God, O'Brien! It's a . . . it's a *scalp!*'

The freelance fighting-man turned back to him, wearing a tired but mischievous smile. 'I know,' he said with a nod. 'It used to belong to Corporal Robinson.'

BANDIT'S GOLD

Alex Frew

When Joe Flint meets Matt Harper and Pete Brogan, he is enticed by their tales of gold and mystery. They tell of a legendary Mexican leader who funded his reign during the Civil War through a criminal network. Drawn in by the promise of fortune, he follows his new friends. But along the way, they are attacked. Flint learns too late that he has put himself in the hands of madmen. Will he find his fortune? Will he even get out alive?

THE SMILING HANGMAN

Owen G. Irons

The town of King's Creek is in uproar. Young Matthew Lydell has been found guilty of murdering Janet Teasdale, daughter of a local banker. Lydell is to be hanged. But the town marshal has been delaying proceedings, and sent for a hangman from the county seat. The hangman arrives quietly, unnoticed. He tours the jail and the town, smiling, always smiling. What secret lies behind that smile, and what intentions does he have for the Colt riding on his hip . . . ?

FUGITIVE LAWMAN

Jethro Kyle

Down on his luck in Chicago, Dale Carnak ends up applying for work with the Pinkerton National Detective Agency. Spotted by an old acquaintance, he is swiftly hired, and agrees to the risky assignment of infiltrating the Fraser Gang — even participating in a train robbery. But a series of misunderstandings sees Carnak become a fugitive, on the run with the rest of the outlaws. Then the bandits begin to suspect that their newest recruit is not who he claims to be . . .

THE PROVING OF MATT STOWE

Lee Lejeune

Ranch hands Matt Stowe and his younger brother Jed are dissatisfied with their tedious, poorly-paid work on the Snake spread. Then the ramrod offers them the chance of earning a little extra cash by travelling to Dodge City and gathering information on the movements of Ned Shanklin, a psychopathic criminal suspected of involvement in cattle rustling. Accepting the job, the Stowe brothers set out for Dodge. But they're riding headlong into far more trouble than they'd bargained for . . .

COMANCHE DAWN

Jake Shipley

Out patrolling the flatlands, Texas Ranger Cal Avery comes across a wrecked stagecoach and two corpses. Nearby lies a survivor of the incident, thrown clear when the coach went over. After tending to the woman's injuries, Cal offers to accompany her to Camp Sheldon. Little does he know, however, that in his absence, the unscrupulous Jake Elkins has accused Cal of shooting two men in the back — and now there is a warrant out for his arrest . . .

THE LAW IN CROSSROADS

J. L. Guin

Jack Bonner, former lawman, has retired to the small town of Crossroads, Texas. But when a rogue gunman shoots up a saloon, Bonner feels obligated to investigate, as there is no lawman in town. He reluctantly agrees to take on temporary marshal duties. Things go sour when Z Bar ranch owner Horace Davies hires a known gunman instead of cowboys, turning the Z Bar into a haven for outlaws. And when Davies offers a reward for Bonner's demise, Jack goes into action . . .